NO MATTER THE COST

THE EPIC STORY OF RJ AND YORK
BOOK THREE

SUSAN MAY WARREN

Soli Deo Gloria

NO MATTER THE COST

The worst has happened—but RJ refuses to believe it, and until she has proof, she's going to keep searching for answers.

But the past won't stay quiet, and it'll take a trip back to

Russia, to York's past to find the answers that will save lives...the kind of answers that dig up the secrets and lies that have embedded York's life.

And even then, does RJ have what it takes—with, or without the man she loves—to save the world from Martin's terrible plan?

The riveting conclusion to the epic adventure of RJ and York!

CHAPTER
ONE

P rague, Czech Republic

She should be on her honeymoon.

Which definitely would not have included a wild night out at Prague's hippest nightclub, Music Club Lucerna, located a ten-minute walk from beautiful Old Towne Square. The bar was originally a theater, built in the early 20th century, and it still had the jutting front stage and massive balcony.

And, tonight, the music pulsed out into the dark, rain-slicked street, shiny with bright lamplights under a star strewn sky.

Yes, a night for romance.

Maybe. Hopefully. If this night went the way of her wildest dreams.

RJ had managed the entire walk in a pair of spike-heels, a mini-skirt, a gold-sequined vest and a hot, long auburn wig.

1

She wasn't sure why she'd opted for the disguise, but if York wasn't indeed alive and waiting for her at said club, then...well then she didn't want his killer to know he'd been made. At least not until she could figure out his identity.

And from there, she'd put his fate in the hands of her friend Roy. He'd left them shortly after York's disappearance, saying he had an emergency in the States.

Whatever that meant.

Roy did things that she didn't want to think about. Maybe none of them were sinister or dark. Maybe that was just her crazy imagination. But once she got the information on York's killer, Roy would know what to do with it, and then...

Well, then York's murderer might find justice.

Except York wasn't dead. No, really. He wasn't dead.

RJ knew it in her heart.

"The place is already hopping." The words issued from Ziggy, her voice close to RJ's ear, and she practically shouted them over Corona singing, "The Rhythm of the Night".

Oh, goody, they'd happened upon 90's night. A DJ stood on the stage, surrounded by techno gear, wearing headphones, one of the earpieces propped behind his ear as he bopped and sang along.

On the floor in front of the stage, bodies gyrated and danced hard, their sweat seasoning the air, along with the bitter redolence of too many spilled mixed drinks.

"Do you see York?" RJ shouted back. Even the balcony was packed, partiers leaning over the edge, fists pumping and singing.

Ziggy shook her head. Her short black dress, high heel, over the knee boots, her long, silky black hair tied up in a high ponytail, light brown skin, and tall, lean body, the woman seemed at ease in the place. Then again, she was a cohort of Roy's who had practically materialized out of the darkness a few weeks ago in Heidelberg, Germany, saving RJ's life.

"I'm going to look around!" Ziggy motioned her intent with her finger, circling above her head. "You keep your eye trained for Raisa!" She pointed toward the long silver bar that ran under the length of the balcony.

Right.

Raisa Yukachova, the leader of the Oden, aka, the Orphans, a super-secret, super lethal group of assassins who were behind the attempt on York's life.

She bit back acid pooling in the back of her throat. This had to work. York had even thrown down the plan before he'd chased a killer off a cliff ten days ago. *Fulfill the contract. Get paid and trace the money back to the source.*

The contract he'd been referring to was the one on his life, of course. It had seemed like a brilliant idea a week ago. When York was alive and breathing and bigger than life.

Maybe not quite so brilliant now, ten long days later. Ten days that she'd woken up every morning in disbelief. As she waited for her cell phone to ring.

She had no other plan but this one, but she'd gotten it into her head that York was waiting for her to do exactly as she'd said.

So, she'd confirmed his kill. Manufactured a bulletin that she spread through Interpol, and onto the internet, including a picture of a dead York, thank you photo shop.

And then she waited.

Now, as her heart beat, she could almost hear him, her name, whispered deep inside. RJ...

She even looked up, at the crowd on the balcony, as if the man she loved might be hidden in the shadows.

Nothing, and she was living on dreams.

Focus. She made her way on her stilettos toward the long

bar looking for a woman-slash-killer who'd been in the wind for nearly a decade. Somehow her sister, Coco, had unearthed an old, somewhat sketchy picture of the woman from the dark web, but who knew how accurate it was.

Still, the Russian, former Bratva moll was a knockout, despite the fuzzy picture. Long blonde hair, tall, shapely, with dark blue eyes that could probably stun her target long before she put a bullet through his heart. Just looking at her picture sent a shiver through RJ.

York was right—maybe this wasn't a world they wanted to be a part of. Oh, how stupid she'd been to pull them back into it.

And the first thing she planned to do when she found him was tell him that. *I'm sorry, York.*

Patrons clogged the bar, young Czechs shouting at the overworked bartenders, women flirting with men in tee-shirts and dress pants, a few in suits. The women wore heels, skin-tight dresses, a few in leather jeans and tank tops. All manner of hair color, tattoos and piercings, a few with blue, or hot pink hair. RJ felt downright pedestrian, despite the crazy glittery dress and so much makeup her face felt shellacked.

But if that's what it took to find her husband's...

Not killer. Because he wasn't dead. The Lauchtenland Coast Guard hadn't found a body.

And besides, she'd been down this road with York before, and the first time, they'd actually *had* a body.

So. There.

In her heart, she believed that York might also be tracking down the source of the bounty put on his head via the Orphans. According to York, the hit order was protected by a passcode, only removable by the owner, once the hit is confirmed. From there, the money was paid out electronically.

But according to Coco, the owner of the hit contract had

parked his money in a highly protected account, and the only way to retrieve the payment was through a manual hand-off that contained the encrypted password.

How she'd obtained that information, RJ didn't know, but Coco had once been a white-hat hacker for a Russian general, so there were plenty of things they didn't talk about.

All that mattered was that the owner of the contract, or at least his or her representative was here, somewhere in this mess of gyrating bodies, and as "Right in the Night" boomed over the speakers, RJ scanned the room for something that looked clandestine.

Forget about your troubles...

The room pulsed, drinks held high as people sang along. Bodies moved past her, the crowd tight, clogged. She maneuvered to the end of the bar and looked down the row in the dim light.

There. Her heart nearly choked her.

A woman stood at the end of the bar, dressed in a suit coat, over a tank top, her blonde hair pulled back, almost painfully, staring into a glass of dark liquor. A black Russian—the thought flickered through RJ and she laughed, then decided that the entire spy thing had gone to her head. Sheesh.

Still, the woman lifted the glass, took a drink, oblivious to the crowd around her and then...

Then she stared right at RJ.

RJ blinked. Swallowed. Stilled.

What—?

But if the Orphans were after York—certainly they'd know his wife, right?

Even if she was wearing a wig?

Okay, breathe. But all her Sydney Bristow fantasies congealed in her head in a brutal moment of what-if.

She didn't even know how to do a roundhouse kick.

Raisa lifted her mouth in a smile, then looked away, taking another drink.

Calm. Just...

She turned, not to run, but only move into the shadows, and somehow smacked right into a man behind her.

For a second, the build of him, the wide shoulders, the dark blond hair—her breath caught.

But the man was too young to be York, and he didn't carry York's scar, the one that ran across his jaw. And, he smiled at her, something flirtatious.

York didn't have a flirtatious bone in his body. He meant everything he said.

"Sorry," she said.

He said something in Czech and moved to take her spot at the bar.

She turned around, her gaze landing back on Raisa.

Except, the woman had vanished.

No—

No. RJ stifled a word and pushed back to the bar, next to the man, and leaned in.

Raisa wasn't among the crowd at the bar.

Where—?

RJ shoved away, out into the crowd, shouldering and elbowing through the mass toward the other end of the bar. But the DJ was shouting something in Czech, and the crowd shouted back, pumping their fists, then cheering. Apparently, something big was happening on stage, but she pressed toward the end of the bar.

There. She spotted the woman.

She stood near a doorway, her back to the wall, one leg up, her stiletto against the wall, the drink to her lips.

RJ would simply slide into a space near the wall and watch. And when the handoff went down—

Someone shoved her from behind, and she turned, but the person kept pushing, and it took a second, but she realized the crowd behind her was rushing the stage.

What—?

Screams lifted, the music throttling up over it, an electronic pulse, the words of the chorus shouted from the dancers-- *Where do you go*—and deep in her mind, she knew this song, more than just for the dance beat—

Her feet caught on a dancer, and suddenly she was falling. She reached out, caught another person, but they shoved her away, and just like that, she was on the floor.

People screamed, tripping over her, and she put her hand over her head as she fought for her feet. "Help!"

A few hands grabbed for her, but her rescuers tripped, nearly falling, and they managed to kick her, trip her again, and this time, someone fell on top of her, trapping her. She kicked, pushing, fighting, but another person tumbled onto her.

The body shucked the breath out of her, and she gasped, pushing at the shoulders, or hips or whatever trapped her chest.

Help.

Talk about being in over her head.

Around her, more people were screaming, whatever was happening on stage reaching a crescendo, and just as the song clicked in her head—

Hands reached out and pulled the bodies off her. People scattered, made an opening.

And then someone reached down from behind and pulled her up.

Curled his arms around her waist.

Then he swung her up into his arms.

7

And for a second—too long of a second, her imagination went wild. Tall, handsome, broad shoulders—

He wasn't dead—

"RJ? Are you kidding me?"

She looked at the man holding her, aware that she'd also put her hands around his neck, clamped them tight.

And then the song landed.

The theme song to the blockbuster action movie by superstar actor Winchester Marshall.

Her cousin Winchester Marshall, handsome, strong and tonight's surprise guest at the Lucerna Music Club.

"Win?"

"Hey, Couz. What are you doing here?"

Her mouth dropped open, even as he carried her to the stage. Then he put her down, his arm around her, even as the crowd cheered.

The hero, saving the girl on the floor.

But all RJ could see was the empty place where Raisa had been.

And a scan of the room as Winchester spoke to his audience—in Czech, no less—told her the terrible truth.

There would be no honeymoon.

She had to be kidding.

Seriously.

No, please tell him that the redhead in the audience wasn't *his* redhead.

His wife, RJ.

York stood in the middle of the crowd, his eyes on the stage, trying not to feel punched.

Except, he'd been reeling for the better part of ten days, so maybe it was more being freshly punched.

Breathe.

He took a step back, toward the shadows, and tried to unravel just how he'd gotten to the moment when he'd nearly blown his hard-fought, pricey cover and revealed that indeed he wasn't dead, but very alive.

And very angry.

His jaw tightened as Winchester Marshall—of course it was Winchester Marshall who'd rescued RJ—wooed the crowd in Czech.

The jerk had miraculously shown up nearly everywhere he and RJ had been over the past three weeks, from Paris to Italy, even Lauchtenland, a tiny country where York had convinced RJ to marry him.

Where, finally, he thought they'd found their happy ending.

But then he'd played prey for the United States CDC director, a man named Grey, and everything went terribly off the rails.

He could still feel his heart leave his body as he ran, arms windmilling, legs kicking, off a cliff over the dark and frothy North Sea.

He'd landed in the cold grip of the water, sank fast and nearly didn't make it to the surface. When he did, the current had grabbed him, flung him out to sea and if it hadn't been for a fishing boat hauling him in like Jason Bourne, he might have turned into fish fodder.

He'd feigned amnesia even as he put the pieces together.

Sure, he knew a bounty sat on his head, but he'd been attacked not as York but as the CDC director, which meant that maybe someone was *still* after him.

Which also meant that his beautiful wife was still in danger.

But if he was dead...

So, he did it. Again. Played dead, although in his defense, the first time, he hadn't remembered dying. Just waking up as a guy named Mack.

If RJ hadn't tracked him down and reignited his memory, he'd still be Mack, small town bartender, slinging brews and burgers in a tiny pub in Shelly, Washington.

But RJ had come looking for him, and the rest was history.

He should have known she'd repeat her hope for rescue. Or maybe, she was just following up on his words to her that seemed now somehow prophetic. *Fulfill the contract. Get paid and trace the money back to the source.*

He still had a few contacts, and he'd reached out to a friend named Artyom, a former hacker for the FSB, now a very discreet private contractor in Germany, and discovered that indeed, Interpol listed him as deceased.

Huh.

It did give him some movement, because it wasn't hard to procure from Artyom the necessary papers and credit cards from a previous alias, and soon he was Dayton Smith, from the UK, just a tourist here in Prague, thank you.

Not tracking down Raisa Yukachova. Not intercepting an email (thank you, Artyom) about meeting her contact here to receive payment for York's death.

He'd killed a day or so in Old Towne Prague, wishing that RJ was with him as he strolled over the Charles Bridge, with Wenceslas Castle peering down from its spot on the hill. He'd purchased a pork knuckle and ate it as he wandered the cobblestone streets. Watched a street busker play his violin and threw in a few bills to his open case.

Yes, RJ would like it here. The history, the aura of

romance in the lilac trees. He thought he saw her a couple times, her dark hair wispy in the wind, thought he heard her laughter, but it was simply the longing of his heart.

He could nearly feel her in his arms when he stood at the window of the Fox Hotel, that overlooked Prague's Old Town Square, almost taste her on his lips, so close was the memory of her.

Wow, he missed her. Which is why, probably he'd conjured up the idea that the redhead might be her when she arrived tonight at the club. She wore a glittery gold dress, and heels and the outfit was so ridiculous that he'd dismissed the crazy idea.

Then, he'd spotted Ziggy, and a fist formed in his gut.

"RJ..." he'd actually growled her name, and for a second, despite the chaos of the club, the raucous music, and the gyrating crowd, he thought she heard him. Looked up, right at him.

He'd stepped back from the balcony, his heart racing. And sure, he wore a disguise—had dyed his hair black, wore a printed tee-shirt under a suit jacket, a pair of runners. And he'd let his beard grow.

Could hardly stand himself in his own skin.

Still, he held his breath, as if that might make him disappear.

She'd sighed, then headed to the bar.

He breathed out. So, the money he'd dropped for his new outfit had paid off. And maybe he'd stop feeling guilty about the few accounts he kept in secret around the world for just this sort of thing. He'd thought of draining them, but frankly, hadn't had time.

Providence.

It was then he'd spotted Raisa. She stood in a pair of black pants, stilettos, wearing a tuxedo jacket, nursing a drink. Probably a black Russian, her favorite.

Funny that he could still remember that, but he'd been dredging up a lot of his past recently, and there she was, too. He kept his gaze pinned to Raisa, watching then as she looked up, then moved away from the bar and under the balcony where he couldn't see her.

Almost as if she knew.

He moved toward the stairs. The crowd was thick enough that if he played it right, she wouldn't spot him. But he'd see the hand-off, and he'd know who wanted him dead.

And then...well, he wasn't exactly sure what he'd do with that information.

Or rather, refused to admit to himself what he'd do with it.

Because this needed to end. Him, looking over his shoulder. Him fearing that someday he'd come home and find RJ....

Find RJ beaten and hung and murdered just like Claire. And if they had children...

He couldn't lose another son.

York's chest tightened as he moved toward the stairs.

And that's when the screaming started. The DJ on stage took the mic, shouting into it, and despite the fact that York didn't know Czech, he knew something big was hitting the stage.

He stopped, and everything inside him froze as Winchester Marshall took the stage. The actor-slash-wannabe spy wore navy blue silk dress pants, a white shirt that just might be a size or two too tight, the sleeves rolled up his forearms, the perfect scruff of whiskers and a pair of aviator glasses like it might be broad daylight.

The woman beside him nearly lost her knees. She screamed, reaching out for the guy.

Listen, he wanted to say, I've met him. He's not so great. A little too smug. And the one time that York had taken him down, into a pool, the guy had hardly fought back.

So, not exactly the spy he played on the silver screen.

The crowd surged toward the stage as Winchester started to dance, grinning, pointing to a few women who screamed appropriately. He was clearly here for a publicity stunt, maybe for his new movie.

Whatever.

York was turning away when he spotted the crowd, or rather, spotted the redhead in the crowd, being pushed forward.

Tripping.

Then she fell. "RJ!" He surged to the rail. She was struggling to get up, fighting— "RJ!"

Shoot. But what was he going to do?

He lunged toward the stairway and flung himself down the steps, out onto the floor, pushing, elbowing—

And just like that, Winchester was there, pulling her up. He must have seen her from the stage, but he parted the crowd and pulled her right up into his glorious arms.

Okay, stop, because maybe the man—her second cousin— had saved her life.

Then Winchester walked with her, right onto the stage.

The crowd cheered, as he set her down, put his arm around her.

But RJ peered right out into the crowd, as if searching for—

Oh. No. Raisa. York turned, searching.

Gone.

Maybe through the lobby—

But even as he started toward the front door, he jerked to a stop.

Ziggy stood just a few feet away, scanning the crowd.

Shoot. The lobby was well lit, and less crowded, and he didn't stand a chance of her not spotting him.

Except—so what? If she knew, then she could tell RJ and—

And RJ wouldn't stop looking for him. Even if he told her not to.

Not if she thought he might be in trouble.

So...he looked around. Spotted a younger man standing with both his arms around a brunette, her back to his chest. His wallet bulged in his back pocket.

Too easy.

He spotted another man wearing a suitcoat, his arm up over the shoulder of a woman he was trying to woo.

This could work.

York headed toward the younger man, tripped and knocked into him. "Sorry," he said, as he pushed off him.

The man frowned at him, and York held up his hand.

Then he spun and walked past the man making his move. Dropped the wallet into his suit pocket.

Returned to the younger man. "Sorry again—but I think that guy took your wallet."

The younger man turned, checked his back pocket, then looked at the man York pointed to. "Hey!"

York blended into the crowd, watching the argument, then the scuffle erupted. A few more people joined in, trying to calm the men down.

Ziggy's attention turned to the altercation, and York slipped past her, fast walking, head away, until he hit the door.

He practically ran out into the street.

Lights splashed on the sidewalk, the beat of the music pulsing into the night. Overhead, the sky had cleared from today's rain, and a thousand lights shown down, watching.

Raisa, where are you?

He took off down the street, toward the nearest subway

station. Rounding a corner, he cut along a dark street lit by a singular lamp on his way to the nearest station.

The lamplight saved his life. The shadow appeared in front of him, the figure behind him, and he didn't have time for a groan. He whirled, and neatly deflected the knife headed for his kidneys. He caught the wrist, dug his fingers into the wrist.

Heard a laugh.

"Oh, Voron," Raisa said, her blue eyes glittering, her smile hiking up on one side. "I knew you weren't really dead."

He stilled.

She dropped the knife. It clattered on the cobblestone.

Then she shook his grip away, stepped up to him, put her hand around his neck, and kissed him.

CHAPTER
TWO

P rague, Czech Republic

She had so many questions bulleting around her head, RJ didn't know where to start, so as soon as the door opened to Winchester's posh, Four Season's Royal Suite, which of course overlooked the glittering Vltava river, she let go with the first one.

The craziest one.

"Are you following me?"

Winchester had said nearly nothing to her after his heroic save of pulling her off the floor, carrying her to the stage, and setting her down beside him like he might be a knight in shining armor.

To the crowd he was, because they'd gone absolutely, ridiculously ape over him, cheering to whatever he said, a few women even opening their necklines, or showing off a shoulder, begging for autographs.

Crazy.

All the time she'd stood there, searching for Raisa.

No. Searching for...well, York. Because she couldn't help but believe, deep in her bones, that he was there.

Maybe she was the crazy one.

Especially when Win now turned to her, frowning, his mouth open. "Hello. You're following *me*."

"Not even a little. I had no idea you'd be there."

Ziggy had walked to the window, was staring down at the scenic view of the red-topped roofs, the lamplights on the Charles Bridge. "I think you could jump from here."

RJ looked at her, frowned.

Ziggy turned. "What?"

Winchester flicked on the overhead light and the view of the river vanished in the glow of the room. He walked through the room, Lake and his other bodyguard, Declan, on his tail. They shut the door behind him, and one joined Ziggy at the window, checking the locks.

Posh didn't seem the right word to describe the red velour, gold-tasseled sofas, the glass chandelier that dripped from the center of the room, the thick draperies, and gold-etched mirrors. The place even had a fireplace.

An overflowing fruit and snacks basket sat on the dining room table in the next room, a bottle of wine chilled in a table cooler.

"Then it's just a coincidence that the one place where...I... decided to go for a night out is the same place where you just happen to show up?" RJ said now, glancing at Ziggy.

Sure, Winchester might be her cousin, and had spent time with them in Italy, but he wasn't privy to the latest on York.

Namely, that he *wasn't* dead. Please.

In fact, Winchester was one of the people who had testified to York's demise, appearing for the cameras as he talked about seeing him go over the edge of the cliff. "He was chasing someone—it looked like a waiter—and then he simply grabbed him, and they went over the edge."

He'd been instrumental in setting up tonight's sting.

Even if he didn't know it.

Even if they'd failed.

Days later, she'd spotted him at the palace—a friend of Queen Gemma's—so certainly he would have heard that they hadn't found a body.

She'd left the country without talking to him again, so absorbed in her brilliant plan.

Now what? She ground her jaw, trying, suddenly, not to cry.

Win looked at her, his mouth tightened. "Are you hungry?"

She shook her head.

He walked over to the table. "I have way too much food here, and champagne and—"

"I could go for a burger," Ziggy said.

RJ glanced at her. "Really?"

Ziggy lifted a shoulder.

"Lake, can you or Declan order a burger from room service," Win said.

Declan headed toward the phone.

"RJ?"

"I'll take a Diet Coke," she said. "And I'd give my right arm for a donut."

He laughed, and it didn't sound at all like a guy who might be behind York's murder. Because, in truth, that was what started rolling around her brain from the minute she landed on the stage with Win.

And since arriving in his suite, one thought had forced itself to the top of her mind.

York was right.

And all she had to do was go back to that moment, two plus weeks ago when he'd tackled Winchester into a pool in Tuscany. When, after RJ defended Win, York stopped trying to drown him, let him go and stomped away.

When she'd run after him into a private garden only to find him not only dripping but hot with fury, and accusation. *It's just too coincidental that he's here. With you. Again.*

At the time, she'd defended Win. Told York it could be explained. That Winchester Marshall was not trying to kill her, or him...that he wasn't a real spy, but an actor.

Now, as he uncorked the champagne and poured it into two glasses, his Italian silk suit coat open, his hair perfectly tousled, wearing the right amount of charm in his smile...

Yeah, he was a suspect all right.

He came over. "Champagne?"

RJ shook her head. Ziggy took the glass, glanced at RJ. Her tight lips and solemn expression suggested she might be thinking the same thing.

Win sat on the sofa. Crossed one leg over the other. "My press agent had this event on my calendar for weeks. I think I even mentioned it—"

"Not a word," RJ said. "You said something about a commercial, and maybe a publicity event—"

"Well, it's not like I need to run my schedule by you." He tilted his head.

It might be the first time she'd ever seen him annoyed.

"No, of course not. It's just..." She glanced at Lake, back to Win. "I was surprised is all."

He let out a breath. Uncrossed his legs and sat forward. Held his champagne glass in both hands. His voice softened.

"Why aren't you back in Montana? After everything that happened...I would have thought you would have gone home."

Oh. But he was right, probably. A normal, grieving widow wouldn't be dressed in stilettos, and something slinky, attending a 90's dance party in Prague. Yes, he had something there.

She looked at Ziggy.

And got nothing. Ziggy's eyes widened, something RJ didn't expect from the woman of intrigue.

So, she defaulted to the truth. "York always wanted to bring me to Prague. He'd been here before—and so had I, but only briefly. He wanted us to see it together." And just saying that out loud burned her throat, choked her. Her eyes filmed. "I thought..." She swallowed.

Win put his glass on the table. "You thought you'd honor him by fulfilling that wish."

A tear slipped down her cheek, and she wasn't sure it was an act. She nodded.

Win drew in a breath, then pursed his lips and nodded. "I get it." He raised an eyebrow. "I'm not sure he'd dig the red wig and the gold dress—"

"He would have loved it," Ziggy said.

RJ looked at her, and the woman smiled at her, almost a sisterhood in her expression.

Win nodded, then picked up his glass and leaned back into the sofa. His chest rose and fell as he considered her.

And she considered him back. She liked Win. He had made her laugh in Italy, while she tried not to worry about York, and his whereabouts. And in Paris, where they met, he'd purchased her coffee.

Coffee at a shop where this entire tragedy began, where, for the first time, she'd spotted escaped American traitor Alan

Martin. Of course, she had to grab York, embroil him in the search for Alan and his sinister plans.

Which had included the kidnapping of a German scientist who turned out *not* to be a German scientist, the crashing of a plane—that happened to belong to Win, so that was again weirdly coincidental, and the stopping of an EMP attack on another plane. This one happened to be connected to the CDC director, who apparently had a hit out on him, something they discovered after a hotel they'd hoped to meet him at blew up.

Win hadn't been there for that, of course, because he'd been at a winery in Tuscany, working on a screenplay and scouting a location for an upcoming movie. But he'd shown up a few days later in Lauchtenland for the Queen's Rosendans, a summer Garden party.

Where York had died.

So yes, she stared at Win, sizing him up.

"Do you need a place to stay? The suite had three bedrooms. Enough for you and Ziggy. I can get separate rooms for Lake and Declan."

Oh.

Ziggy spoke up. "We have a hotel in Old—"

"Yes," RJ said. Then she leaned down and slid off her stilettos. "I'm exhausted, and I've never stayed in a Royal Suite, so..." She smiled at Win.

He smiled back. "I'm so sorry, RJ. I know he wasn't a fan, but he was a solid guy and he desperately loved you."

Aw. And now her throat really tightened. She looked away, wanting to refuse the words of sympathy, repel them from her heart.

Because he couldn't be dead.

But he hadn't shown up tonight, had he?

She reached up a hand, wiped her cheek. "Thank you, Win."

"Does your family know?"

Coco knew, of course, and she was married to Wyatt, so, "Yes."

"I'm surprised that one of them hasn't shown up here."

Frankly, she was too. Because, being the youngest, and only girl, she was used to their overwatch. "It's okay."

The door opened and Declan came in carrying a bag. "Had to ask the kitchen to special order it. They were closing for the night." He set the bag on the table. Then he handed RJ a can of Diet Coke.

She opened it as Ziggy sat down and opened the bag.

"I'm going to go talk to the front desk and secure a couple rooms for my guys." He got up. Declan turned to go with him.

"I'll go," Lake said. "You secure the windows in the back bedrooms, Deck."

The man nodded and disappeared into the next room.

"What are you thinking," Ziggy said quietly as the door clicked closed behind Win.

"I'm thinking that this is the perfect opportunity to search his room," RJ said and popped up.

Ziggy put her burger down. "What are you hoping to find?"

"I don't know, but I can't get past the feeling in my gut that York was right—Winchester is somehow mixed up in this entire thing. From Paris to Italy to Lauchtenland to tonight. He keeps showing up, and it's weird."

Ziggy stood up. "I'll keep an eye on Declan. You nose around Win's room."

RJ was already at his door. Or at least she hoped it was his.

Yep. King-sized fluffy bed with enough pillows for a rugby team, red brocade drapes over the headboard, and two dozen fresh white roses in a vase on the bureau.

A laptop sat on a Queen Anne writing desk, the icon spinning.

She beelined for it. Wiggled the mouse.

A picture of Winchester's family appeared on the screen. That, she didn't expect. Three men and a woman stood around an older couple, standing on a white sand beach, the blue sky arching in the back.

A password prompt appeared.

She hadn't a clue what to type. And what would she find, really, a portal to the dark web where he'd posted a notice for the killing of the man she loved?

She pressed the sleep button, and the picture disappeared.

So yeah, she hadn't a clue what to look for.

She searched the desk and found nothing questionable. A watch, a pair of glasses, charger cords. In the garbage was an empty gum wrapper, and a cardboard container. She picked it up. The packaging for a USB drive. She dropped it back into the bin.

Clearly, she was letting her imagination—her desperation—lie to her.

She closed her eyes, her hands on the back of the desk chair.

Why would Win have a reason to hurt York?

He wouldn't, that's what.

And behind that thought, nudged another.

What if York was really dead?

No...No—

Hands landed on her shoulders, tightened. "What are you doing here?"

She jerked, turned.

Lake stood behind her. Tall, blond hair, built, the man frowned at her.

Oh. And of course, her stupid brain simply emptied of anything useful. "I...uh..."

"Did you find my cell phone, Couz?"

The voice came from the door, where Win stood, his hands in his pocket. He came in, his gaze landing on Lake. "I asked her to retrieve it from my desk. I seemed to have lost it."

Lake looked at her, back to Win. "I thought you had it earlier tonight."

"No." He patted his pants pockets. "I seemed to have misplaced it."

"I didn't find it," RJ said.

Win made a face, kept walking into the room. "Maybe it's in the bathroom."

He walked by her and flicked on the light. "Yes. There it is."

In a moment he returned, holding it. "I thought it was somewhere in here." He walked up to her, hung his arm on her shoulder.

Smiled at Lake. "I think we're good here, Lake. Early day tomorrow—we're headed to Munich. Flight leaves at nine."

Lake nodded, cast another look at RJ, his mouth tight. "Good night."

RJ nodded at him.

Win waited until he left the room, then let her go and turned to her. "So. What aren't you telling me?"

He wouldn't call his response shock, really, because he'd had plenty of women kiss him without notice—including his wife RJ. But usually, those women weren't international assassins with Bratva blood and a history of killing the men they kissed.

Men like Alexander Latvenko, a Pakhan of the Bratva, a former lover who'd been found with his neck slashed in his own bed.

Naked.

So, yeah, the moment Raisa pulled him to herself and pressed her lips against his, York stiffened, caught her wrists, and jerked away.

Held her tight. "Stop."

She was still pretty. Her hair tied back, those blue eyes large and luminous. Maybe some lines around her mouth, but just as beautiful as the day she'd shown up on his doorstep, uncharacteristically shaken and a little panicked.

He might have been the same way if he'd killed a mob boss. Even if he did deserve it, given the bruises on her face, her arms. Probably her body, but he didn't ask. Just took her in.

Hid her.

Found her the first of many new identities.

Sent her to a safe house in Hungary.

She'd vanished after that, clearly getting her feet under her.

"Don't kiss me."

She smiled at him, leaned in and pretended to bite him, her teeth clamping down inches from his face. "What? Scared of me, Voron? C'mon."

"Not scared," he said, still holding her hands. "Although I don't want to kiss you and find a knife in my throat."

"Kidneys. I'd let you die slowly, so you could tell me your secrets." She winked. Then she shook out his grip. "But I'm not going to kill you, York. Because you're already dead." She held up a USB drive. "And right here is my payment."

He reached for it, but she yanked it away and tucked it into her shirt.

Right.

"Although it does seem that maybe someone *lied* to me." She stepped back and picked up the knife that lay on the cobblestones. Pulled up her trousers and slipped it into a leg sheath.

"Not a lie. The world—everyone but you—thinks I'm dead."

He stayed a distance away, just in case she decided to lunge at him. But she snapped the sheath closed and let her pantleg drop.

"But you're not dead, are you? So, still a lie."

He stared at her, her blue eyes glittering. "I might as well be, as long as there's a bounty on me."

"Bounty's gone."

"Until I show up, alive."

She lifted a shoulder. "You could stay dead."

He could. And the thought tightened his jaw. But, in truth, it might be for the best.

"But you won't."

He stared at her.

"For the very reason you won't kiss me." She smiled, held up a finger and advanced toward him, pressing it to his chest.

"Maybe I don't *want* to be kissed by you."

"Oh York. You always wanted to be kissed by me."

He pursed his lips. Turned away from a memory. "I was angry, and grieving."

"Yes." She pressed her hand on his chest, then, and sighed. "I know."

He caught her hand. "Really. Raisa. I'm not here for that."

She pulled away. "I know. You're here for her. To find answers so you can protect her."

Everything inside him seized.

She laughed. "Oh, your face. York." She pressed her hand to his cheek. He kept an eye on the other hand. "You do love her."

He swallowed.

"The redhead, although my guess she isn't a redhead, is she?"

He had nothing.

"I saw her watching me, at the bar. And then you—you nearly threw it all away. This little ruse. You nearly went after her when she fell."

A stone had formed in his throat, and he swallowed it down.

"I saw it all. Saw the fear on your face." She let her hand drop. "By the way, I like the beard. Different. You look like a lumberjack. But I miss your golden locks."

She looked like she might be reaching for his hair, and he caught her wrist again. "Enough. I need answers from you, not flirting."

She jerked her wrist free. "I can't help you."

"Yes, you can. I need to know who put out that hit on me."

She drew in a breath, considered him. Then, slowly, she shook her head.

"Why not?"

"Because, the moment we receive payment, the file is deleted. It's gone, York. I can't tell you who put the bounty on you."

He stared at her, hating how his insides turned to ash.

"Did you see him?"

He said nothing.

"The man who handed off the device?"

"I know who you meant."

She laughed. "You didn't. You missed him."

For a crazy moment, the urge to reach up, put his hand around her throat, maybe squeeze away her laughter surged through him.

He stepped away from her, ran his hand across his mouth.

"Then his ruse worked."

What—?

"That movie star. He came on stage at exactly the right time."

York stared at her. "Winchester Marshall is...he put out the bounty?"

She held up her hand. "I didn't say that. I don't know who put up the bounty. I just know that I completed the transaction the same time he took the stage." She lifted a shoulder. "Could be a coincidence. Could be deliberate." She slipped her hands into her jacket pockets. "Guess we'll never know."

He just stood, chest rising and falling.

He *knew* it.

And RJ was on stage with him. She could be with him right now.

"I can't believe you'd do it again."

York frowned at Raisa. "Do what?"

She started to walk. He fell in beside her.

"I remember you after your wife and son died..." She glanced at him, and for a moment, he saw the past in her eyes.

Saw the man who opened the door to her, let her inside. Hid her.

And then, weeks later, tried to lose any memory of the man he'd wanted to be in her arms.

"We were both broken, York," she said, and for the first time the charade, the bravado stripped from her voice. "But I doubted that you'd ever make it back."

They'd come out to the wide boulevard that led to Wenceslas Square, the neo- renaissance National Museum glowing under the bright lights that bathed it. Wind stirred the night, stars sprinkled overhead.

"I nearly didn't." He wasn't sure where those words came from, and now he looked away.

"And then you met her."

He glanced back at Raisa. She was looking at him, something of sadness in her expression. "I'm glad. You were a good man, York. I knew that. That's why I came to you."

Oh. He never felt like a good man.

Until recently. Until God had reached in and redeemed him.

Until he let go of his anger.

"But I am surprised you'd do it all again."

"Do what?"

"Love someone who could die because of you."

She might as well have stuck that knife in his kidney, because heat swept through him. And of course, he'd known that, but to have her speak it aloud...

Except, he wasn't that man anymore. He didn't make those kinds of enemies.

Still, he must have groaned because she stopped, turned to him and put her hands on his arms. "Did you ever find out who killed Claire and Lucas?"

He had nothing. Because suddenly she could see right through him to the truth he didn't want to admit.

He tightened his jaw, but he must have gasped because she turned to him. "York?"

"No."

"So. You don't know if you still have an enemy out there."

"An enemy who might have put a bounty on my head."

She met his eyes. Nodded.

He looked away, the words peeling out of him, leaving him raw. "I'm going to get her killed."

Her mouth tightened.

He returned his gaze to her. "We need to find out who tried to kill me."

She wrinkled her nose, a sort of wince. "Actually, York, truth is, you weren't the target."

He blinked at her.

Her hands smoothed his lapels. "Your death was a bonus."

"Then—wait." And his brain must be moving in sludge

tonight because he'd already figured this part out. "Your man was after Grey, the CDC director."

"Mmmhmm."

"And I got in the way."

"Thank you for that."

He gave her a look.

"For the record, I wanted to turn down the bounty." She lifted a shoulder. "You know, because...but it was a nice sum."

"Thanks."

"If it helps, I'll keep your lie."

"It does. For now."

"Does that mean..." She stepped up to him, the glint, the flirt back in her eyes, her hands on his chest.

"Raisa—"

She leaned in, toward his ear, grabbed the lobe with her teeth. Then, "I know you missed me."

Not even a little. "I'm married."

She leaned away. "She's your *wife*?" Stepping back, she shook her head. "Oy. Ladna. Then I guess we'll have to keep you alive."

"Why?"

"So you can live happily ever after." She slipped her arm through his.

"Where are we going?"

"Back to my place. Nothing is ever lost on the internet. We'll figure it out, York."

He didn't know why, but he was strangely buoyed.

She led him six blocks away, to the fourth floor of a five story walk up. Historic, but remodeled, her flat had hardwood floors, original molding, but a classy, stainless-steel kitchen, and overstuffed white leather furniture. A massive fur rug covered the floor, with a fireplace that ran two stories to the ceiling.

A loft overlooked the main room, with floor to ceiling sliding glass doors that opened to a balcony.

He stepped out onto the stone, stood at the wrought iron railing, staring at Wenceslas Castle on the hill, the brightly lit hotels along the river. A lonely boat drifted under Charles Bridge, as lights glittered against the Vltava river.

"Nice place."

She came out to stand beside him. "You should see my place in Paris. Across the street from the Eiffel Tower. It glitters at night."

"I know." He drew in a breath.

"I'll make up the sofa." She turned then, leaning on the railing. "Although, there's room—"

"No." He looked at her.

She gave him a wry smile. "What-ifs."

"Sorry."

"A girl has to try." She leaned up. "For the record, I'm glad you're not dead." She headed inside.

But he stared out into the night, watching as the boat slowly disappeared, leaving a trail of starlight in its wake.

CHAPTER

THREE

P rague, Czech Republic

If she was in a movie, this would be the moment when the killer revealed his sinister identity, overpowered her and strangled the heroine.

She'd live, of course, using a pen or a lamp string, or even some happenstance moment, like a kick to propel him through the glass and over the side of the balcony to the river below.

But this was not a movie, the desk lamp was bolted to the table, and there wasn't a pen in sight. And despite the roundhouse that Ziggy had taught her—mostly as a joke—RJ didn't have a prayer of sending the six-foot two, two-hundred-pound muscled actor through any glass window.

Which meant she simply stood there, rooted, empty as Winchester stared at her, waiting for an answer to his question, *What aren't you telling me?*

32

Ah...um.

A beat. Two. Winchester raised an eyebrow. "Really? You still don't trust me?" He glanced at the door. It was closed, courtesy of Lake, his bodyguard who Win just dismissed. After conjuring up an alibi as to why she might be riffling through his belongings.

So, maybe...

"RJ. I don't believe you're here, dressed up in," he gestured to her ridiculous getup, "whatever this is because you're trying to recreate some fantasy adventure York dreamed about."

Oh.

His mouth made a grim line. He took a breath, ran his hand behind his neck, squeezed a muscle there. "I know York was... okay, I'm not sure, but I think he might have been a spy, right?"

Her eyes widened.

"He did show up with Roy at the house in Tuscany pretty roughed up. And took me out with some serious skills. He could have killed me."

"He wouldn't have killed you."

Win raised an eyebrow.

"Without a good reason."

He cocked his head.

"Fine. He thought you might be trying to..." And she stopped, stared at him.

Because right here, right now, she had a choice. Trust Win, her cousin, the man who'd now saved her, twice in one night. Or not. And continue hoping that she might unroot something.

And not get herself killed along the way.

"What?" Win said now.

She drew in a breath. "It was just...still is, so coincidental."

He continued to stare at her. "Um, you lost me. What is coincidental."

Right. "You'd better sit down. It's a bit of a story."

So, he did. Right there on the edge of his bed. She turned around his desk chair. Here went her future. If she was wrong, she might be the one who ended up in the river.

She hoped Ziggy was still awake and could hear her screams.

Ziggy! "Did you see Ziggy?"

"No."

Weird. She got up. "I need to find her."

"Why? Maybe she went to bed."

"Actually, she was on lookout while I searched your room."

He didn't even flinch at that. "I see. I wondered what you were doing in here. Did you find my secret stash of romance novels?"

She had nothing.

"Kidding. It's a family story about my sister—anyway, why were you searching my room."

She drew in a breath.

"Oh. Wait." He leaned forward. "Do you think I had something to do with York's death?" He frowned. "He ran off a *cliff*."

She got up. "I need to find Ziggy." Because the last she'd seen of her friend, she'd been trying to distract Declan, and something didn't feel right in her gut.

"Fine. And then, you'll tell me what is going on?"

She stopped at the door. Considered him. He'd also gotten up. And, he not only looked worried, but confused.

Then again, he was an actor. "Maybe."

She opened the door and stepped out into the main room. No Ziggy. The balcony was dark, the lamps the only light in the room, pooling on the white carpet. "Ziggy?"

No answer. She walked into the dining room, flicked on the light. She didn't know what she expected to see, but of course Ziggy wasn't sitting at the table, waiting in the darkness.

"Maybe she's in the bedroom," Win said and headed down

the hall. He knocked and opened the first one, an inner bedroom. Flicked on the light.

RJ looked past him, even as he stepped inside.

"She's not here," he said.

She continued down the hallway to the final bedroom. It too was dark. She flicked the light on. Stood in the quiet room.

Where—?

A banging on the window jerked her and she turned, her heart nearly leaving her body.

Ziggy stood at the French doors, knocking on the glass.

What?

Win had followed her in, and now went to the doors, unlocked them and opened them.

Ziggy came inside, her eyes lit. "Just in time. I was about to have to break something. Someone locked me outside."

She looked at Win who held up his hands. "I was with RJ. But maybe one of the bodyguards didn't know you were outside. Declan was closing down the house, if I recall."

Ziggy narrowed her eyes at him.

"Lake found me searching Win's room," RJ said quietly. "Win covered for me."

"Hmm." Ziggy said.

"I don't know what you two think I did, but I promise, I wouldn't—"

"Put a hit out on York?" Ziggy said.

Oh. She went there. Okay then. RJ stared at him, looking for a tell-tale response.

Win just blinked at her. Then, "What?"

Silence.

Ziggy looked at RJ. "So, do we believe him, or do we throw him over the balcony."

RJ wasn't sure she was kidding. "I think we believe him."

"Yes, believe me," Win said. He again held up his hands. "I'm not a spy, I just play one in the movies."

If he was trying to be funny, it didn't work. Silence. Another beat.

"Fine. RJ bring him up to speed. I'm going to make a call." Ziggy left the room.

RJ heard the other bedroom door closing.

"I'm listening."

"Okay, like I said, it's a long story. And I'm hungry." She pushed past him and headed back to the dining room. Rifled through the food basket and emerged with a bag of trail mix.

Returned to the sofa, and sat on it, opening the bag.

She searched for the M&M's even as Win sat down on the other sofa. "You mentioned a coincidence. What coincidence?"

She considered him for a long moment. In theory, most of the information she could tell him was public record, albeit suppressed. But if she hoped to find York, she needed someone else in the hunt. So, "How familiar are you with the plot to kill President Isaac White?"

"By the VP-elect, Reba Jackson? Just what the news, and Isaac has told me."

She stopped mid-bite, a raisin in her hand. "Isaac?"

"We're friends. I'm a big supporter, but even before he ran, I knew him from my director, Lincoln Cash, who knew him from Montana. White owns a ranch there, and so does Lincoln. Lincoln brought him in to consult on a movie I did years ago, in my early acting days. Isaac and I hit it off. He taught me a few things—I like doing my own stunts, and he taught me some skills to keep the fight scenes realistic."

She nodded, finished chewing. "So, York and I were the ones who figured out the plot."

Win's eyes widened. "You saved his life?"

"Not me, exactly, but a few of us. He formed a private investigation team after that, and York and I are on it."

"So, you were spies."

She blinked at him. "Are spies. York's not dead."

Win frowned. "RJ—"

"No, Win. I know it sounds crazy, but I've been through this before with York. He actually lost his memory last time, but...no. I don't believe he is dead. He's up to something, and that something includes *pretending* to be dead."

A beat, then, "You really believe that."

"With everything inside me."

"Because you're spies, and that's part of the spy game."

"No. We gather intelligence. And stop potential terrorist attacks. And generally, help the president protect the country."

"So, spies."

Right. "Maybe. But some of us are real spies, some of us just...gather intel."

"York."

"Real spy, in Russia, for a decade."

"I knew it." He nodded, almost to himself. Then he laughed. "He must think I'm an idiot."

Oh. She dug through her mix for more M&M's. "I think York just knows what it feels like to really risk his life. And maybe that's the point he's been trying to make to me all along." She sighed. "Something I should have paid attention to instead of trying so hard pretending to be something I'm not."

Silence. "Is that why he doesn't like me?"

She looked up. "Well, you did steal our reservation on the night he wanted to propose."

Win made a face. "Sorry."

"It's okay. But that was the start of it. You, in town. Me, running into you at the coffee shop, and our field trip to the next shop. While I was there, I spotted a man named Alan Martin."

Win shook his head.

"He was the mastermind, with Jackson, behind the assassination plot. And he was heading for federal prison when he escaped. Two days before I saw him in Paris."

"He escaped? How?"

She drew in a breath. But even this information was a well-known rumor. "There's a working theory that inside the CIA is a rogue group of operators who are working with the Petrov Bratva, trying to take down this administration." She found the rest of the M&M's.

Winchester simply stared at her. Then, "Wait. The Russians?"

"Mmmhmm." She popped them in her mouth, then sealed the bag. "They partnered with Jackson to kill White." Again, an easy rumor to uncover. Still, she weirdly lowered her voice.

Win blew out a breath. "Wow."

And this part wasn't exactly top-secret. Especially since Win had been privy to so much of the aftermath while they stayed together in Italy. "And we thought it was all behind us when, right outside the coffee shop in Paris, I spotted Alan Martin. We have history, so I wasn't sure if he recognized me or not, but—"

"I remember you leaving, abruptly."

"I went back to the hotel and got York. When we returned, we saw him with another man—a terrorist leader with the Boko Haram. Martin gave him something, and they separated. York followed Martin—I followed the terrorist."

Win leaned forward, ran his hands down his face. Shook his head.

"I ended up in a village outside Paris, tracking down an EMP bomb." She paused. "The bomb that took out your plane."

He stilled, his eyes wide. "What?"

"Yes. Roy watched it happen."

Win leaned back, his hand over his mouth. Shook his head. "I should have been on that flight. At the last minute, we were rerouted to a commercial flight because they were having plane issues. Lake and Declan went with me—I had an event in Rome. My team was supposed to join me later..."

He looked at her. "Why would they shoot my plane down?"

She didn't want to suggest it, but, "Maybe you were a target, and they missed?"

Silence.

She held up her hand. "Or not. It might have simply been a coincidence."

"I'm starting to agree with York."

Her too.

"No wonder York tackled me into the pool in Tuscany."

"Well, that wasn't entirely your fault. Between Paris and Tuscany, he'd nearly been killed taking out said bomb, and then I was attacked rescuing a little girl from a hospital in Heidelberg. We got separated, and while he was trying to find me, he got the news that a bounty was on his head—"

"A bounty. As in a hit order?"

She drew in a breath. "Yes."

He got up, walked over to the bar and grabbed a glass. Filled it with water.

"The bounty was picked up by an organization called the Orphans, and someone tried to kill him on the way to the vineyard. So, when he arrived and saw you—"

Win had drained the glass. Put it down. "I would have done the same thing."

"He was upset—"

"I'm upset." He stalked to the window, stared out into the

darkness. "And then I showed up at the Rosendans in Lauchtenland."

"The night an assassin showed up. We're not sure if he was there for York, or for Director Grey—"

"Landon Grey, the CDC director? Why would someone want to kill him?"

"They bombed the conference he was at in Florence, remember."

He turned from the window. "No. I do remember you arriving home that same night. You left the next day."

"Because Grey was in Lauchtenland, doing an impromptu talk at Haxton University after he'd met up with an old school chum at the conference in Florence."

"What kind of conference was it?"

"Some international symposia on infectious diseases."

Winchester had returned to the sofa. "There's a world pandemic conference in Berlin next week."

"Yes. Grey is attending. As is the Russian general, Boris Stanislov—"

"The general who was nearly assassinated a couple years ago."

"Yes. By the Petrov Bratva." She didn't add that, for a while there, she was actually the number one suspect. York had saved her life.

For the first time.

"Isaac is going to the conference too."

She looked at him. "What?"

"Yes. We sometimes connect when we're both in the same city. He emailed me when he saw my tour. Unfortunately, I won't be in Berlin but in Munich."

She sat back, wanting to let that information sit in her brain.

Maybe it was nothing. And besides, she was here for *York.*

40

NO MATTER THE COST

Silence, then finally. "RJ? Why did Ziggy suggest that I put a hit out on York?"

Oh. Right. "Because whoever paid for the hit on York was passing off encrypted payment information to the leader of the Orphans tonight."

He swallowed. "And you were hoping to see who that might be."

"Yes."

"And my appearance wrecked that."

"Sorta. I got caught up in the frenzy. By the time you pulled me off the floor, it was all over."

His mouth made a tight line. He got up.

"What is it?"

"It is weirdly coincidental. And I've read enough scripts to know that nothing is a coincidence." He headed toward his bedroom.

She got up, followed him. "What are you doing?"

"Just checking something." He went to the desk and opened his laptop. Wiggled the mouse.

The family picture filled the screen. He typed in a set of letters and numbers, and it vanished to his home screen.

He clicked an icon on the page. "I got a strange notice via text today from my bank."

The icon opened to a page from a Swiss bank and then automatically logged him in.

She stepped up, stood behind him.

His accounts pulled up and she could admit to some shock at his balances. Apparently, it paid to be a fake spy.

"There's a half-million dollars missing," he said, clicking on one of the accounts. "Withdrawn last night, posted today."

It really hadn't made a dent in the balance, but she leaned down just to confirm the number. "Yeah, that's a lot."

"I'm a little embarrassed to admit I don't handle my own

money. I left that to my team...and specifically my assistant, Brielle."

"Maybe—"

"She died in the crash."

He turned. "She was the only one with account information."

"I'm sure you can follow the transfer." RJ sat on the bed. "We did it all the time in—uh—"

He stared at her. "You were CIA."

"Once upon a time. But I do know how to track money. I think I could probably unsnarl this, given some time."

"And then we'd figure out not only who stole from me, but how the money was used."

A beat.

"I didn't pay to have your husband murdered, RJ," Win said, his voice shaky. "I swear it on my life. On family. On my soul."

She believed him. Maybe it was the thinness of his voice, the horror on his face.

Or maybe simply, her heart spoke the truth to her.

"I know."

His jaw tightened. "Good." Then he got up. Blew out a breath. "We're going to find out what is going on, RJ, I swear it."

She didn't know why his words swept through her, right to her bones, but suddenly, she didn't feel quite so brittle.

So alone.

"But to do that, I'm going to need you to come with me to Munich." He turned to her. "I'm so sorry about York. And for however I'm involved."

She stood up, the words almost on her lips. *It's okay. York's not really dead.*

But somehow, over the last hour, the words had become more fragile, more tenuous in her head.

She drew in a breath, her eyes filming. And Winchester must have taken it for grief because he reached out to her, pulled her to himself.

"We're going to get to the bottom of this, RJ. Because that's what family does, right?"

Yes. At least that's what she did. But she looped her arms around his waist, and leaned in.

He closed his arms around her. "I promise, RJ. You can trust me."

I am surprised you'd do it all again.

Of course, Raisa's words hammered through York's head all night, so by the time morning hit, a migraine settled at the forefront of his brain and drove him from the sofa just as dawn slipped down the Vltava.

He made coffee in the Moka pot he discovered in the glorious, gourmet kitchen—he found it hard to believe that Raisa was also a chef—and took it out to the balcony.

The fresh air helped, the sunshine clearing the darkness from his head just a little. And the coffee cut the thumping down to a dull ache.

Still, he could still feel the words, working their way through him, into his bones, his cells. Toxic.

But probably, she was right.

He'd had no business getting married when someone was out there, trying to kill him.

Still out there.

He stood at the balcony railing, watching the river traffic,

SUSAN MAY WARREN

listening to the bells chime in the city, and couldn't help but
wonder where RJ had spent the night.

Where she was, right now.

He couldn't shake the sense that she might be in trouble.
Might need him. Had replayed her falling in the middle of the
crowd a hundred or more times. Woken with a start, and a
sweat from whatever light sleep he'd managed.

So no, he wasn't in great shape when Raisa came out onto
the balcony, holding a cup of tea, playing with the bag as it
seasoned the hot water. "Contemplating jumping? Seems like a
waste of good money."

He looked at her. Frowned.

"Once people find out you're alive. We could do this all
over again."

He pursed his lips.

She smiled, then set the tea, along with a saucer and spoon
on a nearby table. "Don't worry. Like I said last night, your
secret is safe with me."

Probably not. But she seemed serious.

"Any luck finding out who took the contract out on me?"

"I called a friend this morning. He handles the message
board and encrypted emails for the Orphans, so he will dig
around. Apparently, your guy might have left a posting on one
of our general boards, hunting for an operator before the
Orphans picked it up. If so, then we'd have his online name,
and maybe could track it back to an IP address. Maybe."

He nodded, then sat in one of her fancy lounge chairs.

"I did ask him to check into your friend, Grey. Apparently,
the contract on your CDC director has been canceled." She sat
opposite him, crossing one bare leg over the other. She wore a
silky kimono, her hair up in a messy bun, no makeup.

Beautiful and broken. And it occurred to him that once

NO MATTER THE COST

upon a time, he'd been just as broken. *I doubted that you'd ever make it back.*

But he had made it back. Because of RJ. Because of grace, mercy and faith. And was trying hard to hang on to everything he'd learned.

Because he couldn't—just couldn't find himself back there, again. Broken. Soulless. Damned.

"That's convenient." He took a sip of his coffee, letting it embolden him. "Right about the time my contract was fulfilled."

"Could be the same person. Could be your deaths were linked."

"Maybe." He closed his eyes and lifted his face to the sun, the heat stripping away the last of the night.

She moved, and his eyes flew open.

"Just reaching for my tea, Voron. Calm down." She settled back. "But you're getting rusty."

"I'm not the man I used to be," he said.

"Clearly." She raised an eyebrow.

His mouth tightened. "I mean—"

"I know what you mean. There's something different about you. Something..." She narrowed her eyes, even as she put the spoon down, the tea bag wrapped in it. "Settled. Is it the girl?"

He looked at his coffee. "Yes. But..." His gaze returned to her. She was listening. Okay. "It was God."

She raised an eyebrow. "God? Seriously?"

"Mmmhmm."

"You. After everything you've done—"

"Yes."

She went silent. Then, suddenly, looked away from him, blinking hard. "My mother used to pray for me."

He said nothing.

"She was a woman of faith. Attended the Baptist church in

town. Dragged me there when I was little. I learned the songs, the bible stories." She took a sip of her tea. "I found it boring. Or maybe I just wasn't interested, but I fell hard for a guy who ran with the Tambov gang."

"Out of Saint Petersburg. That's how you got involved in the Bratva."

She nodded. "My mother tried once to steal me back. Actually, came to the apartment of one of the Tambov leaders. They beat her right in front of me." She swallowed, closed her eyes. "I knew then that despite her prayers, there was no saving me."

"Raisa—"

"No, York." She looked up and ran a hand across her cheek. "Really. Don't try and save me. You need to save yourself."

"That's not how it works." And his words, suddenly, were as much for himself as they were for her. "We can't save ourselves, even if we wanted to. That's the point of everything God does—to save us."

She stared at him, even as the words settled inside him.

The point of everything God does. And suddenly his friend Roy was in his head, the day York got married, less than two weeks ago. *Life is not meant to be easy. It's meant to be something that makes us cling to God.*

York didn't know when he'd let go. But he definitely felt his grip slipping.

Raisa was still staring at him. "You really believe that God saved you?"

The word swept through him, filled all the brittle, tired places. "Yes. Over and over, including when I took a header into the North Sea nearly two weeks ago."

She made a noise, and he didn't know if it was disbelief or agreement.

In her pocket, her cell phone vibrated, and she pulled it out. "It looks like God is on your side, paren. My guy landed on something." She pushed the phone toward him. "Recognize this man?"

He stilled. It was a school photo, from Moscow State University, some twenty years ago, but the likeness was clear. Dark-brown hair, cut short in this picture, dark-blue eyes, no smile.

He looked just like his brother, assassin Damien Gustov.

"That's Ruslan Gustov," he said quietly.

"Damien's brother?" Raisa asked.

Of course, she'd know the infamous Bratva hit man. "Yes. Why are you showing me this? Is this the man who put out the hit on me?"

And suddenly, it all made sense. And he'd known it, maybe, deep inside. His ex-Bratva contact Gregori had even suggested it that day in Germany, right before he'd been killed—by the Orphans, no less.

He looked at Raisa now, his breath tight.

"He's the face behind the contract out on Landon Grey."

It took a second. "What?"

"My guy traced the IP from the posting. Belongs to Ruslan."

"Ruslan Gustov, Russian scientist and brother to the guy I killed, took out a hit on the CDC director? Are you sure he wasn't after me?"

She lifted a shoulder and texted the question.

It made no sense.

"And he has nothing on my contract?"

She looked up. "I'm typing as fast as I can."

He ran his hand across his mouth, thinking. "Raisa, did any of your people try and bomb a building in Florence?"

She looked up. "Not that I know of. But I do give my people license to be creative."

Coco hadn't found out about the bounty on Grey until after the bomb went off in Florence, so maybe not.

So what did Ruslan want with the CDC director?

"My guy says he hasn't found anything on your contract yet. This was definitely for Grey. But, of course, it's been withdrawn, so..."

"But you have a kill fee."

"If you mean a cancellation fee—"

"Yes."

She smiled. "Of course."

"And you were paid?"

She texted the question. "Why?"

"Because maybe we figure out where that wire transfer came from."

"Oh, I already know that." She glanced at her phone. "Yes, we were paid. But the initial deposit came from a bank in Russia."

He froze. "Bratva."

"Probably." She picked up her tea. "Why would the Bratva want to kill the American CDC director?"

"I don't know." He'd finished his coffee, leaned forward, put his face in his hands. "I just don't. Know."

Silence.

"Then why do you care?"

He lifted his head. She was serious, those blue eyes without guile.

"I...because..." Huh. "It's my job."

"No. It's more than that." She narrowed her eyes, leaned forward. "It's that thing inside you that told me that I could trust you, even in the middle of the night, with me covered in blood. I knew you'd open your door. Knew you'd listen, and hide me, save me."

He swallowed, the memory suddenly brilliant and raw, tasting again the horror, the rage.

The reliving of the very fresh nightmare of seeing his wife

dead at the hands of the Bratva.

"You can't not do something. It's in your blood. And maybe that's why you turned to God because inside, you're the man who does the right thing."

"I've done plenty of wrong things, Raisa."

"No. You've done plenty of just things. Things that had to be done." She leaned back. "That's what separates you and me, York. I don't care who I kill as long as I get paid. You wouldn't kill the wrong man despite how much you were paid."

"I don't kill anyone, anymore."

"Still. I'm right, and you know it."

She finished her tea. Set it down. "My mama used to say that God guards the paths of justice and preserves the way of his saints. Or something like that. Maybe you're one of his saints."

York laughed. "Really not a saint, Raisa."

"Okay, one of his avenging angels then."

He shook his head.

"Ladna. But still, it's something in you." She stood up, picked up her teacup and his coffee mug. "And that's why you can't escape it."

"I *can* escape it."

"Tell me that you're not going to track down this Ruslan and find out what is going on." She stood there, her head cocked, holding the dishware. Then she nodded and walked into the house.

Shoot.

He got up, followed her inside. "I need to know if Ruslan was trying to kill me, too."

She stood at the sink, rinsing the cups. "You know who you have to talk to, right?"

He followed her, picked up a towel. She handed him a mug. Raised an eyebrow.

"Fine. Who?"

"Follow the money."

Oh. No. He set the dry cup on the counter. "Pasha Dobrevich."

"Mmmhmm."

"He's still handling the money for the Bratva."

"Yep."

His mind settled on a memory, years ago. *You're going to cost me everyone, Voron.*

Then come with me.

"For a long time there, I thought he was going to defect. But he refused to leave his daughter."

"Bad choice. They killed his daughter about five years ago." She handed him another mug. "He should have left when you gave him the chance."

He looked at her.

"That was a guess, but I figured as much. You were too much of a do-gooder, even then to leave him to the mercy of the Bratva."

He remembered Dasha. Pretty. Played the cello in the Moscow orchestra. "And he still works for them?"

"Apparently. He had a granddaughter, too, but I think he hid her somewhere." She picked up a hand towel.

"Smart." He set down the cup.

"You know where to find him?"

"I can figure it out."

She leaned back against the sink. Folded her arms over her chest. "You know, if things don't work out with you and the redhead..."

He smiled at her as he handed her the towel. "Take care of yourself, Raisa."

She took the towel and nodded. "Stay dead, Voron."

CHAPTER
FOUR

Nashville, Tennessee, USA

He supposed if he were to live his life as a hostage, spending it aboard a DeWalt, zero-turn riding lawn mower with a 24 horsepower Kawasaki engine with a sixty-inch deck wasn't a terrible way to go.

Tate Marshall powered hard towards the turn, then hit the right steer lever hard, touched the brakes and the machine slid into the corner pocket of the yard like a race car.

Sorta.

If said race car was traveling at nine miles per hour.

But a guy could dream. Which seemed all he could do the past year as he rode out the scandal of his wife's horror—being the daughter of a traitor.

Still, what was a guy going to do when the American paparazzi dissected their lives publicly except hunker down on the Jackson family's massive Tennessee estate and ride out the storm?

He finished the far edge of the back forty field, did a quick scan for the glint of paparazzi cameras lurking in the far woods—the estate had a strict fencing system that was patrolled regularly by the two security guys he'd kept on staff—Rags and Swamp. He couldn't be sure of the loyalty of the others, so he'd let them go. But Rags and Swamp had been Glo's personal protection detail and would have given their lives for her, so Tate trusted them.

Besides, they'd become friends when he served as Glo's protection once upon a time.

Now, as her husband, he was still on the job. Still serve and protect, only this time, up close and personal. Which meant waking with her when she couldn't sleep, and listening to her disbelief, over and over, as she dismantled her mother's lies. And holding her when disbelief dissolved into grief.

It didn't help that the news couldn't stop digging, despite the sealed files, the closed-door trial. Glo barely left the house.

And she'd stopped singing.

That, maybe most of all, left a hollow in him. Because he couldn't escape the idea that if he'd just paid more attention, that if he'd listened to his gut—and most of all, his sister RJ and her suspicions—he would have seen Jackson's jezebel behavior.

He knew liars—or so he thought.

Maybe he'd been the one lying—to himself.

So, mowing lawns and taking care of the pool and fixing the general repairs around the house, and even remodeling Glo's room to be their master bedroom seemed safe, and something to keep him busy.

For now.

He finished the final swipe, the sweet smell of fresh cut

grass rising into the morning. It would be a beautiful June day, the sun high, cloudless sky. Glo would probably spend it by the pool, her eyes hidden behind her oversized sunglasses, wearing a hat, but in that bikini he liked so much. She'd read a book, and avoid listening to the news, maybe talk to her friend Cher on the phone, and somewhere in there he'd find her staring off into the horizon.

Meanwhile, he'd fiddle with the chemicals in the pool, maybe figure out why the engine light kept coming on in his Jeep and pull out the various take-out menus and figure out what to order for dinner.

A real high-tension day.

He lifted the deck on the mower and rode it back to the outbuilding that housed all the landscaping and pool equipment for the property.

The grass near the house glistened with the fresh bath from the sprinklers. The plantation style home, with black shutters and columns and a wide front porch, reminded him of a country club, and sometimes, despite his status as Glo's husband, he felt like the hired help.

Again.

He parked the mower just as Rags came walking in. "Hey Rango, you're up early."

"I like to mow early."

"You just like to stay busy," Rags said. He was dressed in uniform and climbed aboard a four-wheeler. He wore his blondish-brown hair short under his black security hat, was tall and lean, a former division III wide receiver and Army sniper, although he possessed an easy-going country boy smile.

It was better than sitting around, moping.

Letting his failures catch up to him.

"I already checked the back forty."

"Doing my job for me." Rags started up the four-wheeler. He turned to Tate. "I know you're bored, bro, but it won't be like this forever. Hang tight."

"For what?" Tate didn't mean to sound so angry, but, well Reba had derailed everyone's life with her lies and corruption.

Rags backed the four-wheeler out of the outbuilding. "I dunno. But something. God doesn't waste talent."

Maybe he did if that talent failed, big.

"What is that Ranger thing you're always saying?"

Tate sighed. "Surrender is not a Ranger word."

"Semper fi, man."

"You know that's the Marines. And it means 'always faithful'."

"Yep. That too." He slid on his aviators. "Stay the course. Something will come your way."

He bugged out on the four-wheeler.

Easy for Rags to say—he got up every morning with purpose.

Tate shut the doors and walked over to the house. He expected to see Glo sitting by the pool, or even doing laps, her morning exercise routine, but maybe she wasn't up yet. It seemed she'd had a restless night.

The pool sparkled fresh and blue, and he stopped by and picked up the chlorine tester from its box, squatted by the pool and tested the alkalinity.

He tweaked the chemicals then headed inside.

The kitchen was quiet. He opened the fridge and was debating on eggs or pancakes when he heard it.

Singing.

He closed the door. Listened.

Glo's voice. Halting, half-verses followed by a few guitar chords.

What—?

He swallowed down the sudden filling of his chest and headed toward the sound.

She'd remodeled her mother's office into her music room, and he stood in the half-open door for a long moment, watching her.

She wore a tank top, a pair of leggings and sat on the floor, her guitar in her lap, one leg out, a notebook in front of her that she occasionally leaned down to write in. Then she'd shove the pencil behind her ear, her almost white-blonde curls springy around her head, and reattack the song, trying more chords, singing a few bars.

Brand new day, brand new life...

Definitely a new song.

He knocked, and she looked up. "How long have you been standing there."

"Long enough," he said as he pushed the door open. "What's going on?"

"I dunno. I woke up with a song in my head." She smiled.

He stilled, then sank into a chair. "Really?"

"Yeah." Her eyes shined, and he nearly wanted to weep. She was back—at least for a moment. "I could hear the whole thing. I'm just trying to get it down."

"That's...amazing." He slid down to the floor next to her. "Lemme hear it."

"Oh, not yet big boy. It's in its early days. I need some time to work it out."

He put his arm around her, leaned in and pressed a kiss to her neck. "Need some inspiration."

She laughed, pushed him away. "I think I have all the inspiration I need for the moment."

He made a face. "Fine."

"Besides, you're covered in clippings. Take a shower and we'll talk, lawn boy."

He practically ran up the stairs to the former guest room-slash-current Master and jumped in the shower.

By the time he was out and shaved, he found her in the bedroom, standing at the window.

"That's what I like to see. My wife, waiting for me."

She turned, took a breath. "Actually, we need to talk."

Oh. Shoot. He wore a towel. "Do I need to change?"

"Maybe. Maybe not." She came over to the bed. Patted it, and then sat down.

He sat down beside her, folded his hands because this sounded serious and the last thing he needed was to cause trouble.

"I know you've been restless. And that you blame yourself for my mother's betrayal of our country."

Oh. They were going there. "I'm going to need pants."

He got up and went to the walk-in closet, closed the door. A few minutes later, he came out wearing a pair of jeans, no shirt, and barefoot. But at least better equipped to handle this conversation. He leaned up against the dresser. "I don't blame myself. She started her game years before I jumped into the picture. But RJ suggested your mother's involvement months before she was arrested, and I should have believed her."

"You didn't because I didn't believe."

He sighed.

"Your ownly fault here, Tate, is being faithful to your wife."

He looked away. "Maybe. But the president of the United States could have been assassinated right under my nose. And it's that thought that keeps me up at night."

"But he wasn't."

"Still. I wish I could rewind the tape, go back, figure it out—"

"Be the hero."

"Or at least, not be a fool. I guess at the very least, I'd like to apologize to President White."

She nodded, her lips tight.

A beat of silence.

"Glo—?"

"Coco called me."

His brother, Wyatt's wife. Not a usual call, but not out of the realm of possibility, either. Especially since their son, Mikka, was recovering from Leukemia treatments. "Is everything okay?"

"Not really."

Oh. No. "What is it?"

"It's RJ."

He just blinked at her. "What?"

"She's overseas, and...well, York has gone missing."

Again. "And?"

"He went over a cliff into the North Sea and his body hasn't been recovered, but..."

He just stared at her. "What? When? And where did this happen?"

"In Lauchtenland—it's a tiny country—"

"I know where Lauchtenland is. I have a friend who serves in their military, I think as security for one of the princes."

"Yeah, well, RJ and York were there doing something—"

"Dangerous."

"Maybe. Coco was less than forthcoming. But she said that ten days ago, York was chasing a suspect and just...went over a cliff."

He stared at Glo, trying to picture York, a guy who had survived multiple attempts on his life, as well as RJ's, drowning in the North Sea.

Maybe. The guy wasn't invincible. "How's RJ?"

"She doesn't think he's dead, of course. She thinks he was assassinated."

Again, he had nothing. "What?"

"Yeah. Apparently, there was a contract out on him, and RJ is trying to figure out who took it out."

He shook his head. His sister always had this idea she was some sort of spy. Too much *Alias*, maybe. And York didn't help—he dragged her along on all his high-stakes drama.

"So, why did Coco call?"

"Actually, a woman named Ziggy called her. She's with RJ, but she seems to think RJ is in danger. That someone might be trying to hurt her."

Everything inside him went cold. He ran a hand behind his neck. "Why?"

"I dunno. Just...she asked if you'd be willing to go over and help her untangle this mess. And, of course, watch RJ's back."

"And she called you to ask?"

She smiled. "We have a pact, we wives of Marshall men, that says we'll inform each other of possible trouble."

He narrowed his eyes. "Really."

"Kelsey too. Although Knox is much less...well, he's a little tamer than you are."

"You just don't know him."

She laughed. "Well, Kelsey didn't get a call from some mystery woman asking to send him overseas, Mr. Former Ranger."

Fair point.

He drew in a breath. "Should I go?"

She cocked a head at him. "How can you not?" Then she handed him the phone.

He smiled. She smiled back. He took the phone and set it on the bureau.

"I'm going to need a little inspiration, first."

Munich, Germany

The whole thing felt ridiculous.

And not just the roadblocks RJ repeatedly ran into in her search to find the source of the theft from Win's bank account, but also the entire commercial set up.

She'd somehow ended up smack in the middle of a crazy Jack Power's carnival. How the producer for the commercial had secured the massive Marienplatz for an entire day seemed like a feat of great negotiation. Then again, with the mass of tourists pressing against the flimsy fencing that cordoned off the square, the thousands of cell phone shots and selfies taken with the stars between shots, maybe it would put Munich back on the map as a major tourist destination.

The beauty of the Bavarian city had surprised her when they flew over it in a chartered plane, then landed at the airport, some fifty kilometers north of the city.

Red roofed buildings, a number of glorious Gothic and Renaissance churches—two located just off the Old Towne square—a Gothic themed town hall complete with the Glockenspiel clock and enough quaint bakeries and cafes located on its winding cobblestone roads for her to lose herself for a month.

Which, frankly, after two days of trying to focus on her search, with Coco in her ear via her air pods, and Lincoln Cash, the director shouting out instructions to the camera crew, extras and principals, with the smells of roasting pork knuckle and fresh bread seasoning the air, and the growing sense of futility...

RJ just wanted to close herself inside her luxury room overlooking the square, put the pillow over her head and dream away reality.

Put herself back in a castle overlooking the North Sea, tangled in the sheets with the man she loved as they enjoyed their honeymoon.

He couldn't be dead. Because if he was, then those sweet twenty-four hours would be all she had of York. The last memory of a life she should have grabbed sooner.

What a fool she'd been to trade her happy ending for...well, definitely not the over-the-top pseudo spy life Jack Powers lived, but something just as dangerous.

A life that had gotten York killed.

It wasn't lost on her that the bounty on his life had been posted after she'd spotted Alan Martin in Paris. So, if she did the math...York's death was her fault.

And here she was, sitting under the awning of a cafe, drinking an espresso, on the set of a superstar's commercial shoot, being treated like one of the actors. Or at least the special guest of an actor, including a fancy hotel room, gourmet box lunches and dinners, and most of all, living like a woman who hadn't just lost the man she adored.

But then again, York wasn't dead.

"I can't get beyond the holding site where the money was stashed." Coco's voice came through her ear, all the way across the pond where, although it was late-afternoon in Munich, it was dawn-early in Seattle. "If it was transferred out, it's gone dark."

Coco had been at her computer for at least two hours, having ferreted out the routing and account information and crawled through the dark web for a clandestine parking spot for Win's bounty money.

The man had handed over his computer, his passwords, and his complete trust to RJ. And, after two days of nosing around in his files, RJ knew Win pretty well. His private email was full of notes from his family, ones he answered regularly. He also had a number of close friends—a few in the business that surprised her. Like James Caviezel, Kirk Cameron, and Dean Cain. And an email from hockey great Maxwell Sharpe, asking him to appear at some charity event to support research for Huntington's Disease.

She'd searched his other bank accounts, his expenses, obtained his cell phone records, and his credit card statements. All with his permission, but it did feel invasive, despite her need for analysis.

And then she'd found the manifest of the team killed in his crash and started digging into their lives. Just a handful of people—his assistant, a media rep, the pilots, and flight crew, another bodyguard.

She'd even asked Win about them. He didn't know any of them well—just Brielle, his assistant, the one who'd had access to his accounts. And even she had only started two months ago.

"Maybe I should have canceled the commercial, but I have a contract with the studio. And after the two weeks off in Rome, it felt right to get back to work."

Maybe it was good for him, because he'd jumped headfirst back into his role as Jack Powers, donning a suit, helming a hot Maserati and swinging his beautiful co-star Kathryn Canary into his arms.

She guessed that it didn't hurt any of them to put on a brave face, play at surviving life.

Now, RJ turned back to Coco, and her discovery. "Maybe we can go there, pose as the owner of the account?"

"The IP is located in Switzerland, but it has no hard location. The site is used for wire transfers, the owners identified only by numbers. And to access the funds, the password is a

SUSAN MAY WARREN

fifty-two-character long chain of numbers, symbols and letters."

"So, not easily hackable" RJ imagined her sister-in-law sitting in her pajamas, while her son, Mikka ate breakfast cereal on the long table beside her in their gorgeous flat that overlooked Seattle's Elliot Bay. This time of year, Wyatt would be home, too, but about ready to head to summer hockey training camp.

"With the right algorithm, maybe, but it would take a while. But this is why they hand off the password via hard copy. And not the back of an envelope, but probably a USB drive."

RJ stilled. Shoot—where was her brain? "I saw an empty wrapper for a USB drive in Win's garbage can at the hotel."

The roar of the crowd jerked her away from Coco's response and she lifted her gaze away from the computer, searching for—

"Oh my."

"What?"

RJ shielded her eyes as she looked up to the three-hundred-foot tower to the Neues Rathaus, or new town hall, an impressive feat of Gothic architecture that boasted a three-hundred foot tower. "I mentioned that this is a cologne commercial, right? For the Jack Powers brand. I think it's called Captive."

"Seriously."

"Oh, I've been looking into the names of men's cologne—there's one called Guilty, by Gucci, and Sauvage, by Christian Dior."

"That's the one that Johnny Depp sells."

"I don't think he sells it, Coco. He's just the face. Like Win is the face for Captive."

"The name is a little creepy."

"Tell that to the thousands of people standing in the

square watching him rescue Kathryn Canary from the tower. And from what I can tell, he's going to attach to a wire and zip line down to the square holding her in his arms."

Indeed, he had practiced once, swinging down from the three-hundred-foot tower, strapped in with a harness, one arm holding onto the trolley, the other holding Kathryn, also strapped in. Although RJ guessed that those harnesses would be CG-ed out, given their green color.

"You mean his stunt double is zip lining down to the square, holding her stunt double."

"Nope. Win does his own stunts."

"He does not."

"Yesterday he jumped from a plane and landed in a field."

"Tandem?"

"On his own. Apparently, he's a certified jumper. Even asked me if I wanted to jump tomorrow after the shoot."

"Tandem—"

"Of course. But I said no. I'm not crazy."

Silence.

"What?"

"You've done some crazy things."

Only with York.

She swallowed away the thought. "I think they're done practicing. He's lining up for the shot."

Across the cobblestone square, a camera man stood at the bottom of the zip line. A camera was attached to the cable in front of Win, and would proceed them down the ride, to capture his heroic expression.

"And Kathryn Canary is okay with this?" Coco was still clearly trying to wrap her head around the shot.

"I guess so. I think she's a little smitten with Win. Yesterday, after the shoot—they shot the last scene, where they were dining at the rooftop cafe of our hotel—she kissed him. I'm not

63

sure if she knew they were done rolling or not, but Win looked surprised."

"I'll bet. Yep, here it is on her Instagram. Kissing my co-star, hashtag JackPowers, hashtag heldcaptive."

"She's a little high maintenance. Pretty, but she came with an entourage of makeup people, and I think even a massage therapist. Oh, there they go."

From behind a setup of screens and sound gear, Lincoln Cash wore a headset and now spoke into a walkie-talkie.

A shot sounded from the tower.

And then Winchester appeared outside the tower, Kathryn in his arms. He hung onto the trolley, Kathryn's gown flowing around them as they traveled down the line, the brake engaged to slow their descent.

Still as they grew closer, they picked up speed, and the crowd started to cheer. She didn't know if it might be on purpose, but it seemed they were traversing too fast—

Kathryn screamed and tucked her head into Win's chest.

But he had his arm around her, and suddenly the bungee brake kicked in and slowed them down. They hit the end of the bungee, nearly to the bottom and it jerked them back.

Kathryn let go, but Win had her. Even so, she struggled, clearly afraid, and slipped out of his arms. They were nearly to a stop when she fell, landing in a clump on the cobblestones.

Her scream broke through the cheers. She bent over, clawing through the folds of her dress, still screaming, holding her ankle.

Oh. Ah.

"You're making funny noises," Coco said. "What's happening."

"Kathryn Canary broke her ankle. It's...sort of pointing the wrong direction." RJ winced as Kathryn writhed, still screaming.

Win unbuckled his harness, but stunt men and staff rushed to the scene, surrounding her. He pushed his way into the middle and of course emerged with his co-star in his arms.

RJ could only imagine the pictures that would appear on Instagram, the headlines of TMZ.

Winchester Marshall rescues injured co-star.

The sales of Captive would skyrocket.

But he ignored the crowd and disappeared with her into a walled tent.

"What happened? Did he drop her?"

"No. She screamed, and let go, and fell. If she'd just hung onto Win..."

And just like that, her throat tightened.

"Coco, I gotta go."

"RJ?"

But RJ disconnected, suddenly shaking. She closed Win's computer and slid it into a bag.

Then, without a look at the tent, she headed into the hotel.

She didn't know why her stomach churned, why her eyes burned, but by the time she'd reached her third-story room, closed the door, she was biting back sobs.

Dropping the computer, she climbed onto the bed, pulled up a pillow. Put her face into it.

It wasn't the same thing—she knew it. But somehow seeing Kathryn—it had stirred up the idea that she was Kathryn, that she'd done something stupid and made a mess of everything.

A knock sounded at her door. Wiping her face, she got up and opened the door.

Ziggy stood on the threshold. She'd flown with them to Munich, but frankly, RJ didn't know what the woman was doing. She disappeared for long hours, only to show back up. Reminded her a lot of Roy, frankly.

So she didn't ask any questions.

Ziggy had apparently seen her abrupt escape. Wore something of a sad expression on her face. "You okay?"

"Yeah. I don't know why seeing Kathryn getting hurt freaked me out. It's not the first time I've seen someone hurt. Especially doing something sketchy."

"Maybe that's it," Ziggy said. She walked inside when RJ opened the door wider. "Maybe it reminded you of all the things you used to do with York."

She blinked at her, and her throat tightened. "If York is dead, it's my fault."

Ziggy cocked her head at her. "Hardly, RJ. You can't control the evil of others."

"The bounty went up on him after we went to Paris. After I spotted Alan Martin."

"If Alan Martin wanted to kill York, he didn't need you reminding him to do it." Ziggy folded her arms, leaned against the desk. The room was simple, but elegant, with green velour draperies, a double bed, antique parquet flooring, linen-shade lamps and gold fixtures.

And it all freshly reminded her of their honeymoon suite, in a castle turret in a faraway fairy tale land—" York just wanted to propose and go home."

She stared at Ziggy, her expression caught in the mirror behind her. Oh, she looked rough, her blue eyes bloodshot, and she'd lost weight—couldn't remember the last time she ate. "I should have listened to him."

"This old song again." Ziggy stepped toward her. "You need to stop trying to rewrite the past. It's done, the choices made, and here you are. You can only go forward."

She stared at Ziggy. "What if he's really dead?" Her voice emerged in a whisper.

Ziggy drew in a breath.

"You think I'm crazy, don't you? Holding onto this idea that he's alive and..." She stepped away from her, sinking onto the bed. "I just can't imagine a world without York in it."

She closed her eyes, her throat burning, and put her hand over her mouth.

"I know." Ziggy's voice was soft. "I know what it feels like to have your entire world shattered, the one person you love most taken from you. You can't think. You can't even breathe and the only thought you have is...what is the last thing I said to him?"

RJ looked up at her. Ziggy's jaw was tight.

"I pointed out the assassin to him," she said on a wisp of breath. "I sent him to his death."

"RJ."

"And he said...he said...I'll be right back." She drew up her knees, put her arms around them, started to shake. "But he won't be, will he? It's been two weeks. Two. Weeks. And before he'd lost his memory, but this time..." Her vision blurred. "Why wouldn't he contact me?" She looked at Ziggy. "Unless..."

Ziggy swallowed, her face hollow. "I have to tell you something."

RJ stilled.

"At the club, while you were on stage, I was in the front of the house, near the entrance, and for a second—maybe two, I saw a guy who looked like York. A lot like York. He had a beard, and black hair, but he had his build, and his blue eyes, and, I don't know, something about him seemed so familiar—"

RJ had loosened her hold. "What?"

Ziggy held up her hand. "I don't know. And I didn't want to tell you because...because of the hope I see on your face right now. And, because just like that, he vanished, so maybe I was seeing things—"

"But what if you weren't?" RJ wiped her face.

Ziggy lifted a shoulder. "I don't know what is better—for you to believe, or to..."

"Accept the probable truth?"

Ziggy nodded.

RJ leaned back against the headboard, her gaze going to the window. "I'm in between truths, lost in a place where I just have what ifs and wishes."

"You met Mamma Tessa."

"Mmmhmm."

"She's a woman of faith. When I was in my darkest place, she would come to my room and sit with me as I grieved. She used to quote Bible verses—I remember one. Something about God being a strong tower."

She knew this verse. *The name of the LORD is a fortified tower; the righteous run to it and are safe.*

Her gaze went to the church outside, the twin towers rising above the skyline.

From a tower, nothing could reach her.

From a tower, she might be able to see the truth.

From a tower, she might even discover the direction of her next steps.

She looked at Ziggy. "Your mamma was right. My mother said the same thing after my dad died. That was her verse."

Ziggy gave her a soft smile. "I'm going to raid the craft station. I saw cake."

"I could use some cake."

"Of course you could." She headed toward the door. "This is not the end of your story, RJ, just like my grief wasn't my end."

The door closed with a soft click.

She refused to let it echo in the dark corridors of her heart.

Instead, she got up and walked to the window, her eyes on

the soaring twin towers of the Catholic cathedral, Frauenkirche.

No, she wasn't lost. She just didn't see the future. And maybe York was gone. The thought tightened her chest, filled her throat. But God was her fortress.

She didn't know why she had run so far without looking up. She closed her eyes, pressed her hands to her heart. *I'm running to you Lord. Be my tower. Show me the truth.*

Show me what to do next.

She opened her eyes. Below, Win was talking with Lake, standing with his arms folded, nodding at something he said.

As if he felt her gaze on him, he suddenly lifted his gaze, searched the hotel, and spotted her. Smiled and lifted his hand.

She waved back.

Lake looked up too, his eyes unreadable in his aviator sunglasses. But he too lifted his hand.

Then Ziggy walked up and handed them both a cupcake from a cardboard holder.

From her bedside stand, her phone buzzed. She walked over and picked it up.

Coco.

What was it that you said about finding a USB carton in Win's room?

Moscow, Russia

"Stay dead, Voron."

Raisa's advice thrummed in his mind as York sat in the darkness of the pivabar, Petrovich, located deep in the dark alleyways of Moscow. He nursed a bowl of herring and onions, a glass of Baltica 7, and tried not to inhale the secondhand smoke from the man at the nearby high-top table.

This might be a very bad idea.

Especially since, any moment, he expected some element of his past to walk through the door. Maybe someone from the embassy, although most of the people he'd worked with while under the service of the Ambassador had returned stateside. David Curtiss was probably still around, however, with his wife, Yanna, who, ironically, worked for the FSB.

So that was an interesting marriage. David helped him out a few years ago when RJ had been on the run, accused of killing a Russian general.

How things really hadn't changed. They still lived crazy lives, and as he'd sat here for the better part of the last two days, his conversation with Raisa played out in his head. *You can't not do something. It's in your blood. And maybe that's why you turned to God because inside, you're the man who does the right thing.*

No. He hadn't the power to turn to God on his own. That was all the Almighty's doing, ripping away his memory before he could realize the life he was being forgiven for.

And by the time he did, he'd fallen hard for grace. For the new man he'd become.

But yes, he'd always been the guy who wanted to do the right thing. He blamed his missionary parents for that. So maybe it was in his blood.

All he knew was that somehow, deep inside, he couldn't untangle Ruslan's contract on Grey from the contract on his own life. Somehow, they were connected.

And Pasha Dobrevich might have the answer.

So, here York sat at Pasha's haunt, the one where York had tracked him down so many years ago, needing information on the man who killed his family, a CIA asset working with the Bratva who realized that York was following him.

Alexi was easy to blame, but in honesty, York hadn't wanted to believe anything else.

The bar filled up after four p.m., and last night York had stayed until close, nursing the same beer for hours. No Pasha.

But he'd sit here until the man showed up, and if he didn't, well York would have to get creative. Maybe call Coco and see if she could dig up his address.

But Coco would tell RJ, and then RJ would come looking for him, and the last—very last—thing he wanted was her to show up in Russia.

Last time she'd barely made it out alive.

"Are you lonely?" The waitress had come over to his table. She'd gone on shift an hour ago and brought him his herring. Pretty, young, wearing a white shirt tied just above her navel, she wore a skirt and boots, her hair shaved on either side of a long, blonde mane.

"Nyet." His Russian felt a little rusty, but he'd oiled it up over the past couple days. "Vsyo horosho."

She pointed to his beer, and he shrugged, handed it to her. "Spaceba."

It was as she moved away that he spotted the man. Short, balding, and burly, Pasha read more like a thug than an accountant, save for the round wire rim glasses and tidy suit. He shot a look around the room, and York looked away, watching out of the corner of his eye as Pasha slid onto a stool at the bar beside a chum.

They shared a couple shots of vodka. Smoked a few cigarettes. York finished his herring, sipped the beer.

The bar filled up and a woman came in, dressed in pants and a short sleeve silk blouse, she seemed in her fifties, and flirted with Pasha's friend.

Pasha bid them goodnight, kissed the woman on both cheeks then left the bar.

And just like that, the game was on.

York left a stack of rubles on the table—more than enough—and slipped through the crowd, out the door, up the stairs to the ground level.

The smells of Moscow rushed back at him, sweeping him into time. Despite the smells of the city—garbage, gas fumes, the scent of oil and dust—the redolence of deep-fried street food, early season lilies of the valley flowers that seemed to find a way to survive in the nooks and crannies of the Moscow sidewalks.

Here, in the older area of town, the apartments hadn't been given a facelift, some still the squatty buildings of the Khrushchev era, others newer, built in the 80's, with bigger balconies and windows. All, however, had steel bars on the windows, over the doors, evidence of the crime of a new era.

He spotted Pasha lumbering down the street, passing through pools of lamplight. A tramvai rattled by, and York waited until it passed, then crossed the street, hands in his pockets, and quick walked down the sidewalk.

Pasha turned at a corner and he crossed back, then turned, also.

He spotted Pasha heading into a building and picked up his pace, hoping to catch the steel door before it closed.

He didn't exactly have a plan, just running on instinct and hope, maybe a little desperation, and that could account for why he was just a little off his game as he grabbed the door before it closed and hauled it open.

Darkness poured out of the entryway, the light out. He slowed, let his eyes adjust, then stepped inside.

A hand grabbed his neck, pushed him to the wall and a knife pricked his skin right under his ear.

"York. I thought that was you." Pasha leaned in, vodka breath in his ear. "Are you trying to get yourself killed?"

York wanted to turn, to slap the knife from Pasha's grip, but the knife was awfully close to his carotid. He took a breath, kept his voice low. "Already dead."

A beat. Pasha eased his hold. "Who knows you're here."

"Just you."

"No—"

"Raisa Yukachova."

Pasha lowered the knife. York turned.

He could barely make out the old comrade in the darkness. Pasha however, seemed to see just fine as he grabbed York around the back of his neck. He leaned in. "I knew you had a thing for her."

York sighed. "She sends her regards. And she told me about Dasha."

Pasha let him go. His shoulders rose and fell. "Upstairs."

York followed him up two flights until Pasha came to a steel door. He opened it, let York inside, then closed it behind him.

Another steel door barred entry to his flat. "Can't be too careful. Gangs."

Pasha opened the door.

Pasha's wife had died long before York met him, but Pasha kept the flat just the way she'd left it, the same way York had last seen it. Narrow entry, a galley kitchen, a main room with an overstuffed velour sofa and two chairs, a simple table. Golden wallpaper, green carpet. And pictures of Dasha in tiny frames in a cabinet that held an ancient television.

Off the main room was one bedroom. Typical Russian flat, built in the 60's.

He had brokered a deal for the name of Claire's killer at

that very table. And had offered Pasha a way out of his bondage with the Bratva.

He wondered if Pasha remembered as he led York into the room. York stood at the cabinet and looked at the pictures. A few more, also in tiny frames. He picked one up. "Who is this?"

He walked over to York, looked at the picture. "That's my granddaughter."

"Pretty girl."

"She was three in that picture. Vodka?"

He reached into the cabinet, opened it and grabbed a bottle, a couple of lowball glasses.

York sat down at the table.

Pasha joined him. Handed him a glass and picked up his own. "To your death."

York looked at him and Pasha laughed.

Fine. York tapped his glass and threw back the shot. It hit his gut and burned. But frankly, even his bones felt fragile, his body dragging after the last two weeks. It wasn't so long ago that he'd been in a hospital in Italy, nursing two stab wounds.

And then there was the near hypothermia in the North Sea. So yeah, the vodka chased away a few of the creaks.

He put his hand over his glass, however, when Pasha tried to pour him another. "Business first."

Pasha filled his own glass. "Of course. I heard that you returned to America."

"Yes."

"Tired of Mother Russia."

"Tired of the game," he said. He leaned forward. "But the games continue without me."

One side of Pasha's mouth tipped up. "Of course they do."

"You've been sending money to a man named Ruslan Gustov. I want to know why. And where he is."

Pasha threw back the drink. "So, we're there again."

"Ruslan took a contract out on the American CDC director, and the Bratva funded it. And he might have taken one out on me, too."

"Naw. They don't care about America. Or you."

He cocked his head. "That, I don't believe. The Bratva hates me—we both know that. And Anatoly Petrov tried to kill the US President."

Pasha shook his head, reached for the bottle. York caught his hand on it.

"Yes."

A shoulder lifted from Pasha, and he pulled his hand away. "So what? Cold War is big business. Anatoly helps us all. And you, Voron, deserve it."

York sat back, folded his arms. "Ruslan detonated an EMP bomb. Brought down a plane and tried to bring down another one. You don't want us to connect the dots back to the Bratva."

"What do we care about planes? Or EMP bombs?" Pasha leaned back. "Or the brother of the man you killed."

York stilled.

Pasha smiled. "Yes. We know about Damien."

A beat. "I just want to know where Ruslan is. Where you're sending the money. Then I walk out of here, and you never see me again."

"Promises." Pasha sighed. "Nyet."

"Why not?"

"Because last time you talked the truth out of me, my daughter was murdered!"

York recoiled, even as Pasha leaned forward, his eyes dark. "I...I'm sorry."

He took a breath. Looked away. "I should have left with you. Taken Dasha. Taken Ania." His face broke, his breaths rasping. "And now they are gone. They are both gone."

He could probably blame the vodka for Pasha's tears, but

still, York had nothing except horror. His voice fell, soft, gentle. "Did they kill Ania, too?"

"I don't know." Pasha pressed the heel of his hand into his eye, one, then the other. "I changed her name and put her in an orphanage to hide her after Dasha was killed."

Coco had done the same thing with her son, Mikka, when he was four. Three terrible years of their lives while she hid him from danger.

"And then, two months ago, she went missing."

"From the orphanage?"

He nodded. Swallowed. "And that's when a man came to me and told me that I must send them money."

"You paid for the hit on Landon Grey."

"I followed instructions. I don't know what I paid for, but yes, I sent money to the account."

"Does the Bratva know?"

He drew in a breath. Shook his head.

Oy.

And then...wait. "Pasha, how old is your granddaughter?"

"She is ten. I have a...I have a more recent picture, when she was seven." He got up and went to the cabinet. Opened it.

Took out a picture, curled and dusty, hidden away. He handed it to York.

What?

York *knew* this girl. A man named Mads had claimed she was his daughter. RJ had rescued her from a hospital in Heidelberg, and York had saved her from drowning in a pool in Tuscany.

"York. What is that face?"

He looked up. "Your granddaughter is not dead. In fact, she's safe, in Italy with friends."

Pasha took a step back, fell into the chair, breathing hard. "Safe?"

"Yes. And no one but me, and a couple others know where she is. I promise, the men who took her cannot find her."

Pasha stared at him. "I don't believe you."

"I taught her to swim. She has a birthmark on her back, near her shoulder blade."

Pasha took a breath, then suddenly, began to weep, big heavy, bearish sobs.

Oh. Um.

York sat down. Probably he should pour the man a shot, but that didn't feel right.

"Pasha? You okay?"

His meaty hand landed on York's knee. He looked up. Nodded, his face still wrecked.

"Can I get you something? Water?"

Pasha shook his head, took the picture from York. Looked at it, rubbing his thumb across her face. His barrel chest rose and fell. "Ladna. I will tell you..." He looked up. "But only after you do something for me."

York cocked his head. "I don't think bringing Hana here is a good—"

"No. She stays in Italy. I don't want to know where. If I know, they can know."

Tough, but smart.

"No." He sighed and put her picture on the table. "No. I have a different task." He looked up at York, his eyes clearer. "My friend Gregori was murdered two weeks ago."

"By the Orphans."

Pasha cocked his head. "How did you know that?"

"He was marked."

His eyes narrowed and he considered York. "Gregori had a dossier that he hid in his house. Hard copy, not on his computer. It contains...secrets. I want it."

Secrets. "The kind of secrets that kept Gregori alive?"

Pasha got up, picking up the picture. He put it back in the cabinet. "It's time for you to go." He turned. "Bring me the dossier, and I will tell you how to find Ruslan Gustov."

York got up. Felt wrong to shake the man's hand, so he just nodded.

Then he found himself back on the street. And for the first time in days, he tasted the hope of resurrection.

FIVE

Munich, Germany

It had started with a simple yes.

Yes, RJ would fill-in for Kathryn at the top of the tower as they retook the zip line scene. Because of course, Kathryn, trying to keep up with Win had refused a stunt double for this short commercial shoot.

Which meant that any double that resembled Kathryn Canary would have to be found or flown in from across the ocean.

And Lincoln Cash had only reserved the square for two days.

So, after Ziggy coaxed RJ back down to the square with lemon cake—oh, she was so easily bought for a piece of cake with blueberries—Cash had asked her if she might be willing to take the ride with Win down the zip line.

Win's idea, judging by the grin on his face. RJ couldn't quite read it, but she guessed it had something to do with their conversation at the hotel in Prague about trying so hard pretending to be something she wasn't.

Or, she could simply be trying hard not to think about Ziggy's suggestion that she'd seen York. RJ had clamped down hard to that suggestion, trying not to believe it was just a terrible hope.

Whatever the reason, she couldn't help but feel the nudge to say yes. Like, weirdly, God might be answering her prayers about what to do next.

Which is why she found herself later that night, as the sun began to set behind the red-roofed buildings and towers of the Marienplatz, harnessed to Winchester Marshall, his muscled arm around her waist, dressed in a silky evening gown, staring at the ground some three hundred feet below.

"And really, this thing will brake?"

Win wore a fresh tuxedo, had showered between takes, and was the persona of calm and collected.

Every inch of the spy he portrayed.

And it only made her miss York more.

"Don't worry, RJ. It has double brakes, and the stunt manager double checked it. Just hold on, don't panic and trust me." He smiled down at her, and again, everything inside her missed York.

On the street below, Lincoln spoke into the radio where at the apex of the tower, the stunt coordinator rechecked their harnesses. Then, "Ready to roll?" he asked.

Win looked at her. She nodded.

"We're a go."

Somehow, she managed not to scream, managed to hold onto Win and hold her smile, not let the fear rise up and throttle out of her.

They fell with grace, precision and as the zip line slowed, Win's grip around her tightened until he landed in a half-run.

He set her down on the pavement to the applause of their audience, from the production crew to the fans lined up against the barriers.

"Well done!" Win said. He held her arm. "You okay?"

Okay? She might have left her heart behind at the top, but the rush of adrenaline in her lungs from the height, the feeling of soaring made her at once overwhelmed and yet strangely empowered. "I'm great."

He smiled down at her. "Perfect. Because tomorrow you're going skydiving."

He'd unhooked her harness, and then they'd taken a shot of her running across the square and piling into his Maserati and peeling away, her hair blowing in the wind.

Living the life she'd dreamed of.

But it wasn't lost on her that it was all staged. Fake.

And, essentially, safe. Nothing like the world York lived in.

That reality found her bones as Lincoln called for a wrap, and later, as she sat with the cast for dinner, the stars arching overhead, spilling across the skyscape of Munich.

No. She didn't want that life at all. She'd wanted the fantasy.

The reality was dark and evil and cruel.

"I've lost my appetite," she said now as she pushed away from the table.

Win frowned at her and rose. "RJ?"

"I just need to lay down." She looked at Lincoln Cash, who was busy chatting with Kathryn Canary. She'd ended up in the ER, her ankle broken and now in a boot. "Thank you for dinner."

He nodded, and she got up, and headed for the hotel, located a few blocks away.

Ziggy got up also. "I'm turning in." She'd been on set most of the day.

She caught up to RJ. "What's up?"

"I don't know. It feels wrong to be leaping from tall buildings when the man I love is still missing. Or..." She shrugged.

They had turned down a shadowed cobblestone street, lit with lamplights. The romance of summer in Munich hung in the air with the smells of flowers and music from nearby restaurants stirring in the street.

"You know, if York is...if he's gone, he'd want you to keep on living, RJ. He loved you—it was the one thing about him I knew for sure."

RJ nodded, her throat thick. "He did love me." She ran a hand across her wet cheek. "And that love hasn't died. I mean, I feel like he's still with me, still out there." She sighed. "But if he's not, and I'm just carrying the memory of him, then yes... someday I'll figure out how to go on."

Ziggy walked in silence as they crossed a narrow street, continued down the next block. "By the way, I've been talking to friends in my circles, and there's chatter of someone who followed Raisa Yukachova home from the club in Prague."

RJ stopped. "York?"

"I don't know. Maybe. But nothing in the wind about him since then."

She kept walking. "If he's alive, he's probably still in hiding, making sure that whoever took out the hit on him doesn't double back and finish the job."

"Any lead from Coco on the money trail?"

"She found where it landed after it was taken from Win's account, but..." She looked at Ziggy. "I'm an idiot. I found the carton for a USB drive in Win's room. I should have put that together, but—"

"You were looking for me."

"And, I don't know—trying to figure out if my cousin was really a murderer."

"Who's a murderer?"

The voice came from behind them, and RJ turned to see Lake fast-walking up the sidewalk. He caught up to them. "Hey."

"Hey Lake," Ziggy said, glancing at RJ.

"Win wanted someone to walk you ladies home," Lake said. He grinned at them, as if he might be their hero. "So, you were talking about murderers?"

"Just a podcast I'm listening to," RJ said. "My favorite murder."

He stuck his hands in his pockets, walking between them. "I like *Nothing Rhymes with Murder*."

He was a big man, in his mid-thirties, maybe, a military aura to him. "So, are you going to join us tomorrow skydiving over the German countryside?"

Oh. She looked at Ziggy, who raised an eyebrow. "I don't know."

Lake laughed. "Listen, I've been jumping out of planes with Win for the better part of three years. I promise he knows what he's doing." They reached the hotel. "Come with us. Declan was a Navy jumper—he has about ten thousand jumps under his belt. And we'll have a tandem master from the diving company with us. It'll be perfectly safe, and you'll have a blast, I promise."

He left them safe and sound in the lobby.

Ziggy got on the elevator. "So. You want me to search Win's room tomorrow?"

"Tomorrow?"

"When you go skydiving?"

Oh. She folded her arms against a terrible hollowness. The last, very last thing she wanted to do was skydive.

In fact, a day—or a month—with the shades pulled, curled in her bed felt like the only right answer. But if she believed—*truly believed*—that York was alive, then..

Yes. And if this was the only way to keep looking for him... She looked at Ziggy. "I guess that's a good excuse to keep him away."

Ziggy folded her arms. "Atta girl."

Twelve hours later, she wanted to raise her hand and argue. Of course no one would hear her, given the thunder of the wind whipping through the open bed of the tiny charter plane. All the seats of the Pilatus Porter P-6 had been removed, leaving space for six crazy people who would launch themselves out of a perfectly good airplane. Win, herself, Lake, Declan, Stefan the stunt coordinator and the tandem master, Oli, from the company.

Ziggy had better be combing not only Win's room, but Lake's and Declan's and everyone's in his entourage.

"We're nearly to four thousand feet," the pilot yelled to the back.

Oh, that was way too high, wasn't it? Although maybe it didn't matter, really.

A parachute fail was fatal at nearly any altitude.

"You ready?" Win shouted against the wind. He wore a jumpsuit, goggles and a helmet, the wind rippling his face. She wore the same, something she'd rented from the skydiving company. But her outfit also included a camera, attached to her helmet so she could watch everything afterwards.

Just in case she closed her eyes the entire way down, perhaps.

Win sat behind her, and she could feel him tugging on her harness, probably clipping it in. She glanced at Lake. He grinned at her, giving her a thumbs up.

She returned the gesture.

Then she looked down.

Granted, if she weren't about to toss herself out of a plane, she might call the view of Bavaria breathtaking. Surreal. To the east, the Alps rose jagged and white-capped, with massive granite peaks and deep furrows that fell to lush green forested floors. A valley striped with greening fields, twisted roads and royal-blue lakes was dotted by red-roofed houses and a handful of castles.

A fairyland for sure. No wonder the Grimm brothers set their fairytales here.

Win pointed to a massive white castle that sat atop a hill. "That's Neuschwanstein Castle! That's where the Art in Film event is at!"

What event? She nodded, but really all she cared about was finding herself back on terra firms.

The pilot turned back and gave them a thumbs up.

Oh no.

Win sat with his legs around her, her back against his body. Now, he scooted her toward the edge of the plane, the wind roaring in her ears, grabbing at her legs.

Wait—wait—

And for a moment all she could think was—York should be here. With her, his arms and legs embracing her as they flung themselves into the blue.

This was all wrong, and the realization burned, right down to her soul.

"I'm not going to push us out," Win said, shouting. "You have to do it!"

No. She stared out at the world, the blue sky, the magnificent alps, the green valley—

Suddenly, deep inside, she heard a verse, something embedded inside her. Maybe from the day she stood at her father's grave. Or maybe simply her mother, reminding her, over and over, but *God is our refuge and strength, an ever-present help in trouble. Therefore, we will not fear, though the earth gives way and the mountains fall...*

"Let's do this." She gripped the side of the plane—

And then they were out. She might have screamed, but she couldn't hear anything with the roar of the wind in her helmet. Win grabbed her hands and pulled them out, spread-eagle style and her brief training caught up.

They were flying. Weightless, soaring over the earth.

And strangely, all fear dropped away. Just the sense of seeing the world in one gulp, both invigorating and empowering.

They fell for maybe fifty glorious seconds, the world becoming larger. Then Win tapped her arms and she wrapped them around herself, pulled her legs in. He'd deploy the chute and they'd drift.

But, nothing. He yanked and the chute came out, but she heard him say something and looked up.

Froze. The chute was tangled, a mess, spiraling—

He tapped her shoulder. "We're fine!"

In two seconds, he'd cut the chute away. It snapped off, away, and he reached for the secondary chute.

No jerk, like he'd told her to expect, no sudden slowing—

She looked up again, and this time could hear Win's word.

Help.

The chute was torn, right in the middle of the silks, spiraling.

"Win!"

"I'm thinking!"

Think faster! The world had become terribly large—a scream burbled up inside her.

Then, just like that, Lake appeared. He hadn't yet popped

his chute, still falling, and reached for her, grabbing her harness. "Unsnap her!"

What—no!

Lake pulled her arms into his harness, locking them in front of his chest. Then he put his legs around her. "Hold on!"

Hold—what? "No—wait!"

She barely felt Win unsnap her, just the solidness of him vanished as he fell away.

"Hold on with everything you've got!" Lake's arm curled through the back of her harness.

Then he pulled his cord.

She nearly dropped with the force of the chute yanking her up. Lake's legs tightened around her body, his arm gripping her harness and he'd wedged her arms so tightly into his harness she was practically pinned by the G-force.

The world stopped screaming in her ears. Then, silence.

She leaned into Lake's chest, breathing hard.

"I got you, ma'am," he said.

But who had Win?

She glanced over and her heart nearly left her body when she spotted Win attached to the Tandem master, Oli.

She rode in Lake's arms to the field below, and even put her legs around his waist as they hit the ground, him needing his legs to run as they landed. He finally stopped, breathing hard, and she let herself fall to the ground.

Sweet, blessed, perfect ground that she promised never to leave again.

"RJ, are you all right?" Win came running up to her, throwing off his goggles, his helmet, then landing in front of her on his knees. "Are you hurt?"

"I'm fine." She still had a hold of Lake's arm. He had crouched also.

Win sat back in the grass, breathing hard, clearly shaken.

She said nothing, not able to put into words what she was thinking. No, fearing.

But Lake sorted it out with one terrible statement. "Sir. I think someone just tried to kill you."

Potsdam, Germany

He hadn't heard them come in.

York stood against the wall in Gregori's office, the shadows crashing around him as dusk filled the room in the former Bratva thug's estate just outside of Berlin.

A nice A frame, tucked back into the woods, with an outbuilding that held his toys, and a wraparound porch. Half dacha, half new Russian in style.

The silence haunted him, the trees around the property hushing him as he'd picked the lock of the front door and eased his way in. No barking dogs, no alarm.

A terrible red stain puddled on the marble floor, in the foyer in front of the circular staircase. The mirrored walls and ceiling only added to the violence.

He'd headed past it, through the sunken living room with the soaring zebra-painted fireplace, then the dining room with the exotic gold chandelier. The kitchen cabinets were shiny black, and there, on the white tile by the door, was another bloodstain.

Ziggy had mentioned that not only Gregori, but his wife Luda and their granddaughter had been murdered.

He'd looked away and kept moving, past a massive bedroom with a king bed—

and more mirrors—and two more smaller bedrooms until he finally came to a room at the end, right before the theater.

The office.

Zebra carpet on the tiled floors, mahogany desk, with matching bookshelves, and another bloodstain, this time marring the leather chair behind the desk.

A hole in the chair leaked bloody stuffing.

He searched the desk, opening the drawers, looking for a secret compartment or a catch that might open a door in the bookcase, but found nothing.

Nothing except a bottle of Stolichnaya vodka and a .22 Vostok handgun tucked into the back of his middle drawer.

Sorry, Gregori.

York didn't want to believe that this was his fault, somehow, but it was hard to ignore.

Gregori was murdered only a day after he'd met with York. Maybe even hours.

It was as he was searching the bookcase that he heard the voices.

Russian.

Something about how Gregori had a nice house, nice life. Maybe how they should steal Bratva secrets and live their lives in secret.

Probably a bad idea. But he tucked away the conversation and slipped into a closet in the office.

He'd picked up Gregori's gun, but a quick check of the chambers revealed it empty. So he had nothing, Not a gun, not a knife, just his own desperation, and the foolish belief that he could unwind whatever plan Ruslan Gustov, and maybe even Alan Martin, had cooked up to hurt his country.

And as he stood in the closet, listening to the Bratva minions sort through Gregori's office—less delicately than York had—he kept hearing Raisa's words.

My mama used to say that God guards the paths of justice and preserves the way of his saints.

He wasn't a saint. But then again, he wasn't his old self, either. He'd been forgiven, redeemed.

So, maybe a saint, after all. And maybe he'd been kidding himself about wanting to leave it behind.

Because he hadn't exactly returned to RJ, had he? No, he'd run off to Pasha, and now Berlin because she was right.

He couldn't *not* do the right thing.

Shoot.

"Where did you hide it, Gregori, you old donkey."

Of course, that wasn't exactly the translation, but York ignored the rest and held his breath.

The closet was large, with coats hanging in the back, a few boxes on the floor, and, bingo, a safe in the back wall.

Odds were the file was in the safe.

It wouldn't be long before Igor and Ivan, the Bratva brothers figured that out, too.

But if Gregori was smart, he had an alarm on his safe, one that would alert him if someone sneaked in here—

York worked his way over to the safe and turned the dial.

A panel on the safe began to blink. He entered a code—his birthday—and the alarm began to blare. Only, not inside the room.

In the hallway, and the bedroom, and maybe even in the garage outside where Gregori stored his Mercedes Benz SLR Mclaren 999, and a Jaguar XJ13.

Clearly no one had taken a looksee into his garage since his death, something that probably wouldn't last long with the Bratva boys here.

Shouts lifted, and he pressed back into the closet just in case the door opened.

Instead, pounding down the hallway suggested they'd gone in search of the intruder. He blew out a breath.

Fell to his knees in front of the safe and took a look.

A biometric fingerprint security safe with a backup key lock. Something he could get off Amazon, or the German version of it.

York stood up. Gregori would not store secrets that could save—or cost him—his life in a safe that anyone with a decent safecracking kit could open.

It wasn't here.

He opened the door and looked out. The Bratva boys had trashed the office, pulling out drawers, upending the trash. The vodka bottle sat on the desk, the cap off. No doubt one of them had pocketed the gun.

Books lay broken on the floor, a picture fallen, the glass cracked.

The destruction told him one thing.

The Bratva hadn't ordered the hit. Because if they had, they would have not only sent their own people, but they would have secured the file before they finished off their kills.

So then, who?

He'd figure it out later—now he needed to track down the dossier. A quick look out the window confirmed that the boys were outside, and yes, looking in the garage. Hopefully they'd find a cat lurking around.

Meanwhile, York headed for the master bedroom. A quick glance in the walk-in closets netted nothing promising, and he even tried a couple of the hanging pictures.

But he wouldn't have stored it anywhere logical, or even expected. Not when he knew how the Bratva played their games. They'd burn down a house if they thought they could destroy evidence.

Burn. Down the house.

He probably needed to put some giddyap into this search.

He walked into the kitchen, looking for a basement. The

place was up on a block foundation—he'd had to climb steps up to a deck to reach the front door.

So maybe under the house. He went to the back door, waited, but no one appeared, so he eased himself outside.

The wind shivered in the trees. He scurried across the deck and landed below it, crouching in case his movement had attracted attention. Then he peered under the deck.

Just blocks, no windows, no escape, so maybe the house sat on a crawl space.

Gregori's words, their last meeting filled his memory. Gregori, standing in the middle of a beer garden, looking old, pedestrian and every inch a grandfather. And he'd mentioned a granddaughter.

And when York sent his regards, he told him he'd buy her a bottle of Moldavian wine.

Her favorite. And the wine that York brought whenever he stopped by, back in the day when Gregori worked as a double agent.

But Luda loved her wine. So much that they'd spent time in Bordeaux, and the Chianti region of Italy, and Mosel, Germany, and even Catalonia, Spain.

Where would he keep his wine?

Gregori, like many Russians, was a purist—when he adopted a hobby, he went all in. He would have built a multi-zoned refrigerated cellar, with racks for aging and different varietals.

And he would have made it something he could show his friends—and hide from his enemies.

York hustled back in the house.

The alarm still blared, but he slipped into the kitchen, watching the shiny reflection of the cabinets for his company.

They walked by, toward the office again, clearly frustrated with the noise.

He stood in the kitchen, searching for a door, or a floor panel, or—

The island. It had a hinge along the end of the cabinetry, and maybe it was just a door, but...it had a coded alphabet lock just under the edge of the counter.

Right about now is when backup from Coco would help. But a call to her would only alert RJ, and frankly, he didn't have time.

But he did know Gregori.

He bent and put in the four letters of his wife's name.

The alarm beeped. His guess was that he had three tries before he'd have to break it open.

Maybe he should just--There. A picture drawn by his granddaughter of a unicorn hung on the wall by the desk. And, she'd signed it.

Kaija.

Maybe—he crouched in front of the counter and put in the letters.

Another beep.

He sat back, glanced over his shoulder. Hopefully they'd found the safe by now, were fighting with the lock.

Kaija. German name. But in Russian it would be—

Katia.

Bam. The door lock slid back.

He glanced back, but it seemed all clear so he opened the door.

Stairs led down under the island to a cool room, cement flooring. He took them down, closing the door behind him, and finding the light.

The walls to the large room were lined with wine racks, some of the wine behind a wall that clearly slowed the aging process.

Hundreds, maybe a thousand bottles. They were stored cork out, except for a few choices that lay in trays, labels up.

He stood in the middle of the room. In the corner, a small table with one bench suggested a tasting area. That, along with the yellow light that cast over the bottles felt like some kind of eerie monument to a life that yearned to savor.

Probably, however, that was never in the cards for Gregori. Not as long as he had enemies. Even if he did have a way to keep them handcuffed.

York blew out a breath and looked around.

I'll buy her a bottle of Moldavian wine.

His words, but they pinged inside him. Luda was from Moldovia, a country bordered by Ukraine, and Romania to the southwest.

He would do anything to protect his wife. Until, of course, he couldn't, but still, York walked over to the bottles and pulled out a burner phone he'd purchased. Turned on the flashlight in the scroll down menu.

The light scraped along the bottles, and he read the labels. Spanish, French, Hungarian, Italian, German—there, near the end, a rack of maybe fifty bottles, all from Moldavia. He ran the light over them.

Nothing but wine.

He looked at the few wines laying label up. Nothing extraordinary. He picked one up.

The tray it sat on shifted. He put the bottle down, the picked up another, and again, it moved. He emptied all the bottles onto the floor and then pulled out the tray separator.

The wooden floor of the drawer wasn't glued in.

He needed a knife. But he couldn't chance going upstairs—

The corker. He spotted it in a niche near the table. A simple opener, the kind a guy could carry in his pocket.

York grabbed it and opened it. The corkscrew ended in a point.

He used it to pry open the tray.

And in the drawer, laying flat, was a manilla envelope.

He pulled it out and walked over to the table.

Above him, feet pounded on the floor, clearly the Bratva boys getting desperate. Hopefully, he'd pulled the door closed enough.

Sliding onto the stool, he pulled out the contents of the envelope.

Receipts. Printouts of emails. A bank account register. And a tiny black book.

York opened it, and his word slid to a stop.

Names of victims. And, the operator who'd ended their life. Names of public officials and party members. Informants. Bratva leaders, and low-level thugs who had gotten out of hand.

Sparrows, female informants who had squealed stories after squirrelling them out of their lovers, and even ex-pats who had gotten too close to the organization.

And then, his breath caught.

Claire and Lucas Newgate— Damien Gustov.

His knees nearly buckled.

For a long time, he'd thought that the CIA had organized the hit. But he'd...well, he'd had a talk with the man who he'd pinned it on, and long after, years even, had decided that maybe he'd been wrong.

Damien Gustov. Who'd also killed Tasha, his girlfriend, years later, also penned, some lines down.

Damien Gustov, who was dead.

He closed his eyes, a weakness rushing through him.

Dead.

Not following him.

Not haunting him.

It was over.

He breathed out, the cool of the cellar prickling his skin. Now all he had to do was figure out who wanted him dead today. And then he'd be a free man.

He closed the book and slid it, along with the other papers, back into the manila envelope.

Above him, the door creaked.

He shoved the envelope into his belt, in the back, under his jacket and scooted around under the ladder, into the shadows.

"I found something," said a voice, in Russian and York held his breath.

Footsteps down the stairs.

His own voice in his head, *I don't kill anyone, anymore.*

Lord, help me keep my word.

Except, he couldn't see a way out, really.

The first man landed in the room. "Oy," he said, probably taking in the massive collection.

"What do you see?" The question proceeded footsteps down the stairs.

"A secret wine cellar."

The first man joined him. York wasn't so hidden that if they turned, they wouldn't see him. He held his breath.

"There are bottles on the floor here," said the first. He wasn't a big man, but a massive star tattoo covered the back of his neck, his head shaved. The second man bore all the marks of a Russian thug—big shoulders, tattoos on his knuckles, a real Igor.

Ivan, the smaller man, leaned down and picked up a bottle. "Moldavian wine." He spat on the floor.

Igor grabbed the bottle. "You don't know what you're saying." He looked at the label.

It was then that Ivan turned, glanced at Igor, but his gaze fell on York.

Oops.

York stepped forward and pushed Igor with everything inside him.

The man tripped, ran into Ivan who fell back against a wall of wine.

The wall wobbled, clearly not affixed to the wall, and suddenly, wine bottles spilled out over Ivan, hammering him as they crashed to the floor. Igor too fell to his knees, the bottles pummeling him on their way free.

York stepped out, swung around for the stairs, but Igor had turned, grabbed for him.

York spun, kicked out and met Igor's jaw.

The man barely flinched.

York grabbed a bottle of wine from the nearest rack and used it as a bobby stick, taking out the man across the chin.

Igor spun, hit another rack.

More wine bottles, waterfalling upon him, the smell of expensive cabernet rising to saturate the room.

No time to mourn—York scampered up the stairs, then turned and shut the door. Latched it and pressed the code.

The lock clicked.

He took off through the house, hearing the Bratva brothers shout.

No doubt they could break through the doors, later, but by then, York would be back in Russia.

Trading Gregori's secrets for answers.

CHAPTER
SIX

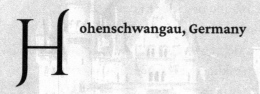

H ohenschwangau, Germany

Despite the fantasy land that she suddenly seemed to immersed in, RJ wasn't going to let anything happen to another person she cared about, and that included her cousin, superstar actor. And not that she possessed any special skills, but another set of eyes watching Win's back wouldn't hurt.

Every cell in her body buzzed, even two days later. In a blink she could find herself falling from the sky, the scream rebuilding in her chest.

If it hadn't been for Lake...

And the tandem master who'd acted as quickly as Lake to save their lives.

Everyone had been rocked, it seemed, especially Stefan, the stunt coordinator from Germany who had personally repacked the chutes after Win's initial jump a couple days earlier. And Declan had signed off on all the packing and had locked the chutes in the stunt trailer.

So, none of it made sense, especially since none of the other chute bags had been tampered with.

"Maybe they were after you," Win had said hours later, back in his hotel room, after debriefing with authorities. They'd retrieved the cut away chutes, and determined indeed, both sabotage in the tangled chutes and in the damaged chute, cut instead of torn. Which turned Win a little shaky.

Lake and Declan had initially refused to leave him, but after checking his room, they'd retired to their adjoining rooms.

Leaving just RJ and Ziggy to help him sort it out.

"Me?" RJ said. "Why would anyone want to kill me?"

Ziggy was standing at the window and now turned. "What about Kathryn Canary? Would she have the means and opportunity to destroy the chutes?"

"Kathryn?" Win said. "Why?"

"RJ did take her place in the shoot."

Win shook his head. "I've known Kate for years. No, she wouldn't do this."

Ziggy ran her hands over her arms, shook her head. "Then someone who doesn't like RJ sniffing around Win's affairs. Maybe she's getting too close to the answers to who stole the money and set up the hit?"

"I wish," RJ said. She stood up. "We have hit nothing but dead ends. Besides, no one knows we're hunting the money trail."

"So, you're back to thinking the target was Win?" Ziggy asked.

"I only agreed to jump the day before. Who knows when the sabotage happened?"

"What about Lake? Or Declan? They have free access into every area, don't they?" Ziggy said. "How well do you know them?"

"Declan has worked for me for five years. He'd give his life for me."

"And Lake?"

"He came on staff about a year ago, but he comes highly recommended. Former Marine. Protected a US Ambassador before he came to work for me."

"And, Lake saved my life, so I don't think it's him," RJ said.

Win blew out a breath and sat down, his hands linked behind his neck. "Maybe I shouldn't go to the Art in Film Awards."

Silence.

RJ met his eyes. "No. You need to go. You can't hide away. It's an awards show, and people will expect you there. And, you're not exactly jumping out of a plane to get there."

"We'll go with you," Ziggy said. She looked at RJ.

Right. "Yes, we will. To watch your back. And if we see anything suspicious, we'll alert Lake and Declan."

He lowered his arms and leaned back against the sofa. "One of you needs to be my date, then, in order to get you in." He looked at RJ. "Sorry, Couz, it can't be you. I can't bear the social drama."

She laughed. "I get that. So, Ziggy, the mystery date. How will I get in?"

"I'll get you a security pass."

"Does that mean I have to wear a black suit, with an earpiece?"

He laughed. "That's up to you." Then his expression turned serious. "But, thank you. I never thought one of my movies would turn into real life."

If this was his real life, then RJ wouldn't mind escaping into it because a further two days later, she found herself in a pair of low heels, a black dress, with an earpiece connected to Ziggy's, holding a glass of cucumber infused water as she wandered through the crowd during cocktail hour.

The early evening event took place under the stars, brilliant spotlights that shown down upon the lower courtyard of beautiful Neuschwanstein Castle, it's creamy white marble walls rising around them. At the apex of the walled area, the main castle rose six stories under a black Gothic roof, towers extending on either side. The entire thing sat on top of a mountain, the walls falling thousands of feet to a river below.

Absolutely magical.

"Did you know that during World War Two, the Nazis hid their stolen art here?" A voice spoke behind her.

She turned. Lake. He wore a black suit, an earwig and looked every inch the handsome bodyguard.

He cast a look over her shoulder, and she followed it. Win, talking with a German actor.

When she turned back, Lake's gaze was on her. "They knew the Americans wouldn't bomb such an amazing place."

"It is amazing," she said. "I heard that King Ludwig went broke building it."

"Mmhmm. It's mostly empty inside, although I guess the throne room, and his bedroom chambers are finished. Apparently, there's even a jungle grotto up there somewhere."

"This was a man with vision." The place could steal her breath, the fantasy of it nearly unbelievable.

"Imagine how the peasants felt, watching him build this place," Lake said with a shake of his head.

She hadn't thought of that. But yes, in the valley far below sat tiny houses in great swatches of farmland. Probably their taxes funded the undertaking.

A nearby band played chamber music. "What is this from?"

"Tannhauser. It's a Wagner Opera," Lake said, and set his empty glass of water on a tray.

"Wow, you really did your homework."

Lake lifted a shoulder. "That's my job." He smiled at her, then walked away as Win moved through the crowd.

Something she should do. So far, she really had no idea what she'd been thinking offering to accompany Win to this event. Like she had the faintest clue what a murderer looked like.

Okay, not entirely true. She had met Damien Gustov once—no twice. The first time he'd shown up on a train platform in Russia. And kissed her.

A message sent to York, and she still shivered at the invasion of it.

The second time, he'd tried to kill York in front of her eyes.

By a miracle, York had lived.

So maybe she did know a murderer. Someone who gave her the willies.

She scanned the crowd. A distinct mix of the glamorous guests and the working-class security and wait staff. Her gaze followed a number of waiters, but no one seemed suspicious.

A bell chimed, indicating that it was time to take their chairs, situated on the upper courtyard. She thought the event might be broadcast to German channels, so all the security were to stay off stage, positioned in the courtyard of the nearby Knights Quarters.

If she wanted to keep eyes on Win, she needed a better view.

As the crowd massed toward the stairs, she headed to the stairs to the right, toward the gatehouse.

She showed her pass to the attendant there, and more magic because they let her through. The stairs took her to the second level, and after a glance over the edge of the railing to the night falling into the valley, she headed along the corridor toward the Knight's Quarters. She found another stairwell and took it up another flight, to the third floor.

The circular stairs kept going, however, all the way to the top of the tower. She considered it, then kept going along the third story corridor.

Stopping along the way, she looked out over the courtyard. Spotted Ziggy and Win seated in the third row, right where the camera could land on them.

Ziggy looked every inch a movie star's date in a shimmery black dress, her dark hair piled up in a tangle of cascading curls, thanks to Kathryn Canary's hairdresser.

Kathryn, who turned out to be nicer than RJ thought, with her willingness to let RJ and Ziggy borrow from her wardrobe.

But a set of lights blocked her view of the entire audience.

She needed a view from the front, looking back.

But she'd have to be higher to clear the stage.

The corridor led into the castle to the back, and she found another set of winding stairs to the fourth, then fifth floor, although, according to the map she'd seen, it was labelled the third floor, the place of the King's personal chambers.

She wandered out into the intricately decorated rooms.

Sconces glowed light into the grandeur of the throne hall, a two story, columned, gold-gilded room void of any furniture. A mural of a knight slaying a dragon hung on the walls, the floor depictions of wildlife.

She walked into a study, with a gold-painted credenza and a mural of the traditional naked women, and then into the dining area, a little tamer, with more gold-gilded walls, swan sculptures and gold-tasseled red velvet dining chairs.

By the time she reached the bedroom, she could hear the music and master of ceremonies speaking in German. The bed was tucked into a corner, with a green damask spread, and an intricately-painted floor. Through the dressing room, she found the drawing room. Parquet floors, a massive gold candelabra, tapestries that depicted some ancient fairytale, complete with more swans.

She walked to the window. It was shut, the glass hazy.

Shoot. But she remembered a balcony—probably upstairs.

The next room stopped her. A small cave, with faux stalactites and a dry waterfall and, through the rocks to the next room, a small room with view to the countryside below.

But, from the grotto, more stairs. She took them up.

And emerged into the massive hall of Singers with its hanging chandeliers and of course, more stunning murals. But at the end, the balcony.

She pushed open the doors. Below her lay the courtyard, the chairs and an unobstructed view of the crowd. The security staff to the left were hidden, mostly by the shadow and lights but the crowd was easily seen, including Ziggy and Win, sitting near the stage. Somehow, she resisted the urge to wave.

Clearly the castle was going to her head.

She scanned the crowd, not sure, really, what she might be looking for and, it hit her that maybe she'd over thought this.

After all, who was going to make an attempt on Win's life at a public even like this? Desperation, even frustration had talked her into this foolishness.

Still, she watched as a handful of actors received awards, giving their speeches in German. Win was up for an award, but it wouldn't be announced until a ways into the program.

Commercial break, and Win and Ziggy got up, and stretched. Win glad-handed a few people.

Ziggy turned and found RJ. "You know that everyone can see you," she said through the earpiece.

"Only if they're looking. Besides, maybe that will deter someone from doing something stupid."

"See anything?"

"Just you, trying to take off your shoes without anyone seeing."

"I'd switch places with you in a hot minute—oh, they're ringing the bell."

Indeed, suddenly everyone moved back to their places. And then the break was over, and the master of ceremonies started up again.

So, maybe she'd head back down. What was she thinking she could do, anyway?

She turned, and that's when she caught movement.

Stilled.

Someone was in the shadows, maybe behind a pillar in the cavernous room.

Oh. Shoot—

"Ziggy, I have company."

Clapping. "You okay?"

"I don't know." She moved toward the stairs.

"Get out of there. I'll take care of Win."

"But—"

"This is why I should have been the one in the black suit. Get. Out."

Right. RJ took off in a run toward the stairs.

Footsteps slapped the wood floor, in pursuit.

What—?

She raced down the stairs, hit the grotto area—

Someone tackled her.

She spilled out onto the grotto floor, then rolled and set her foot into the man's face. The room was dark, only the wan light from the conservatory spilling in, but it was enough for her to kick again, and connect with his nose.

A shout, and she scrambled up.

He caught her leg. "Oh no, you don't—"

Her hands closed around a stalactite and she yanked on it, hoping to free herself.

Instead, it jerked from the ceiling, and she fell back.

The force knocked her attacker over, and she landed hard on her back, the stalactite in her arms.

With a roar, she turned and drove it right into the chest of her attacker. It thumped him, but didn't break skin, but he went down, fighting for breath.

She got up. Turned and kicked him and he swore and tried to grab her foot.

Nothing doin'—she grabbed another stalactite and ripped it down, then used it to again slam into her attacker.

He slapped it away, and it hit the wall.

The entire grotto shook.

Then he bounced to his feet.

Run.

She turned, but he leaped at her. Still, she got her hands around a massive boulder and jerked.

The boulder gave, and with it, the entrance to the grotto shook.

She turned, kicked her attacker in the face, and then scrambled into the drawing room.

The boulders broke away and fell into the room, the entire grotto entrance crumbling.

She didn't look back. Just turned and ran through the bedroom, the study, the antechambers and out to the throne room.

Raced for the stairs.

And nearly plowed over the man barreling up them. He'd hit the landing, was running out into the room when she slammed into him.

His arms went around her, and they launched through the air.

They fell with him on the bottom, cushioning her fall, but with his arms tight around her.

For a second, she just lay there, dazed.

"Are you okay?"

She froze, then pushed the man's arm off her and sat up.

Stared at him. And then, the only thing she could think to say was, "What are you doing here?"

Berlin, Germany

He could almost see the smile on RJ's face. Almost feel the touch of her lips on his. Almost hear her laughter.

She felt so close, he thought, any moment, he might see her walk down the cobblestone street.

But it was just the frame of her, at the forefront of his mind as York sat under a blue canopy of a Bavarian cafe, drinking a cup of espresso, the late afternoon sun gilding the street.

Across said street, and down about twenty feet, the small DKB bank-slash-ATM received little foot traffic, mostly people emerging from the U-Bahn entrance.

He'd been parked here for the better part of two days after his hand off of the black book to Pasha. And, Pasha's assurance of not only the bank's address, but that he'd replenish Ruslan with a fresh advance for him to retrieve.

York didn't know why he trusted him—probably because of the way Pasha had stopped him at the door with a hand on his shoulder. "She's really safe?"

Oh, Right. *Hana.* "If you ever want to know where she is..."

Pasha's eyes watered. "Nyet. She is safe, and that is all that matters." Then he'd squeezed York's shoulder. "Thank you, Voron."

A flight and two days later, York was still rolling that providence around in his mind. Certainly, there was a reason he could puzzle together as to how Pasha's grandchild had ended up in the hands of Ruslan Gustov.

He'd bet it had something to do with the money they needed.

"Anything more for you, sir?" A waiter swing by his table holding a tray of empty glasses.

"Are your pretzels really made here?"

"Of course."

"That. And the keg butter."

Why not. After two days here, he'd eaten nearly everything else on the menu, from the potato soup, goat cheese dumplings, the veal schnitzel, the bratwurst with Bavarian fried cabbage, and the apple strudel.

He was starting to get desperate. And full.

The street traffic was light here, a few blocks away from the Brandenburg Gate. Ironically, the Russian Embassy was also a few blocks away.

He'd also walked the streets, found a hotel nearby, with a rooftop cafe, and booked a room there. Thought about how RJ would like such a place, overlooking the rooftops of Berlin.

He wasn't a huge fan of Berlin—most of the city had been destroyed in World War Two, and the rebuilt buildings were sleek and industrial and lacked the beauty of Paris, or Prague or even Munich and Heidelberg.

"Your pretzel, sir." The waiter put it down in front of him, along with a cup of butter. "Pardon, but who are you waiting for?"

York picked up the pretzel. Still warm. "A friend. He is supposed to meet me, but he's running late."

The waiter raised an eyebrow but nodded. "Let me know when you want your check."

"Now is good." He dipped the pretzel into the butter, his eyes on the U-Bahn door.

A woman came out wearing a short green skirt, black tights and a white cropped shirt, her blue hair up in pig tails. She headed into the bank.

The next few people simply emerged, heading down the street, a man with a backpack, another with a satchel, a woman in red pants and runners.

Pigtails came out of the bank, turned down the street.

He had finished the pretzel, was wiping his fingers when he spotted him. Finally.

Tall, with blond-brown hair, tied back in a man bun, he wore skinny black pants, a green tee-shirt and a satchel over his shoulder.

Not exactly a picture of an assassin, but maybe that's why he hired his services.

He disappeared into the bank.

Gotcha. York got up. Looked for his waiter. Nowhere.

But he added up the bill in his head and threw down enough Euros to cover it, and more, and hustled down the street.

He parked himself directly across from the bank when Ruslan emerged. He wore sunglasses, but York knew him anywhere.

They'd done battle in the back of a van in Italy, for one.

Ruslan seemed in no hurry, walking down the street like he hadn't a care that someone might follow him, might shove him into an alley and start asking questions.

He turned into a coffee shop.

Einstein Kaffe. York stood outside, not sure...then he entered.

The smell reached out and grabbed him up, and despite being full of pretzel, the smell of coffee stirred something to life inside him. Or maybe it was just the sight of Ruslan Gustov, standing at the counter paying for a brew.

Right here, in public, where he couldn't run. Probably.

He walked up behind him. Ruslan glanced over at him.

York stiffened. "We need to talk."

Ruslan frowned, then turned back to the cashier and spoke in German, finishing his order. York got all of it, but he intended on sticking to English. Or Russian.

The man paid, clearly nonplussed at York's appearance, and then went to the end of the counter to wait for his drink.

York followed him to the end. "Did you hear me?" he said in Russian.

Ruslan looked at him. "Do I know you?"

It was a punch, right to the center of his sternum, and he simply opened his mouth. "Um. Yes."

Ruslan frowned. "Sorry. I sometimes forget people."

"People that you throw out of cars and try and kill?"

Ruslan's eyes widened and then, crazily, he started to hyperventilate. "I'm sorry—I'm sorry—"

What—?

"Calm down. Just...breathe." York reached out and touched his back. "You okay?"

The man looked at him. Nodded, then shook his head, then nodded again.

The barista put his coffee on the bar. Ruslan took it, his hands shaking.

"Do you need to sit down?'

He nodded, and shuffled over to a chair, sliding into it and setting his coffee on the table. Wiped his hands on his pants. A sweat had broken out over his forehead.

What in the world—

"I panicked. Alan told me that you were going to steal the device, and I—I panicked." He looked up. "Are you okay?"

York just blinked at him. "I'm...yes. I'm fine—do you remember the boat?"

His mouth widened, along with his eyes. "Oh, the boat. The boat. It blew up!"

"Yes, it did."

He looked down then, shook his head, closed his eyes. Looked up. "You blew up the boat."

York drew in a breath. "You kidnapped my girlfriend."

Ruslan's mouth opened. "She tried to stop me."

"From killing a plane full of people!" He kept his voice low, but added a sharpness to it.

The man shook his head, closed his eyes. "I can't talk to you. I can't—"

York schooled his voice. "Calm down. I'm not here to hurt you."

He opened his eyes. "You blew up my device!"

York glanced over at the barista, to see if she noticed Ruslan's outburst.

Nothing, but then again, they were speaking in Russian.

"I did."

Ruslan looked at him, his expression unreadable. "I made another one."

"Another Marx device."

"I call it Nika. Victory." He got up then, leaving his satchel hanging on the chair, and returned with a handful of sugar packets. Taking off the lid of his cup, he opened each one up, and poured them in, stirring between each one.

York just watched him, sensing something... "Are you okay?"

He looked up at him, frowned. "I'll be fine."

What was up with this guy?

Ruslan put the cap back on. Took a sip. Closed his eyes. "Yes."

Then he put the cup down and took a breath. Met York's eyes. "You tried to kill me."

It sounded almost like another voice, more confidence, more anger.

York leaned back. "You tried to kill *me*."

His mouth tightened. "Yes, well, you were in the way."

He sat, completely nonplussed at Ruslan's confession. "Ruslan, did you...did you ask someone else to kill me?"

Ruslan frowned at him. "Why would I do that?"

Why would... "You just said I was in the way."

"You were. You jumped into the van. You could have destroyed the mission."

He closed his eyes, ran a finger and thumb into them. "Right. Have you ever heard of a man named Landon Grey?"

Ruslan shook his head.

Huh. "Okay, so what mission?"

He leaned forward. "We're going to save the world from the robots."

York froze. "*What?*"

"Yes. They look real, but..." He lowered his voice. "They're AI."

"AI."

"Artificial Intelligence."

And again, York had nothing. "I don't understand."

He sighed and leaned back. "I know. Most people don't. But you'll see. Mads and I are going to stop them."

They were— "*How?*"

"With the Marx device." He frowned, shook his head. "Of course."

"Wait. Are you saying you built the Marx device to protect mankind against AI?"

Ruslan put a finger to his lips, then smiled. "We have a plan."

Ho-kay. He wanted to look around, see if he spotted Alan Martin punking him. "Ruslan, how did you get involved in this project?"

"I was already working on it. But I ran out of money and then Damien said that he knew someone who could help me. He introduced me to Alan. And then Alan brought me Mads."

"Damien introduced you."

"He's my brother."

"I know."

His eyes widened. "You know him?"

"In a way."

He sighed, took another sip. "I haven't heard from him in a long time."

Strange, to see the other side of Damien's life.

"Do you know where he is?"

York considered him a long moment. Then, decided to answer the question ethereally. He didn't need any more ghosts. "Not really."

Ruslan nodded. "He used to tell me, back when I was in school, that someday I'd invent something that saved the world. I wish I could tell him that I did."

"My guess is that he knows."

Ruslan smiled, took another sip. The alarm went off on his watch. He stopped it and pulled out a bottle of meds from his satchel. Popped the top and took a pill.

"What's that for?"

"Oh, you know. Quiet." Ruslan took another drink. "It keeps the voices from talking to me."

Right.

He leaned forward. "So, Ruslan. Tell me, when are you going to save the world?"

He made a face. Looked at his cup. "They won't tell me. Mads says that I'll know when it happens, but I don't want to be too late. Skynet could find us, and then we won't be able to stop them."

Skynet. "Are you...referring to the Terminator?"

His eyes opened. "Is he here? Has it started?" He leaned forward, cut his voice down. "Are we too late?"

Way, way too late. "No. He's not here. We have time."

Ruslan sat back, clearly relieved.

"Ruslan, where is Mads right now?"

He finished his coffee. "I don't know. He left. Told me to watch the device, but I needed coffee. And money."

"Where is the device?"

Ruslan's eyes narrowed. "Why?"

"I just want to know that it's safe. Just in case you need help. That's why I was in the van—I wasn't trying to kill you. I was trying to join you."

He considered him. "No, you weren't."

"You never asked me. You just punched me."

"You punched Alan."

York sighed. "Alan and I don't get along."

Ruslan's mouth tightened. "I don't like him either."

York made a face and nodded. "He's really bossy."

"Yeah. And he's always yelling. Mads is nicer. Most of the time."

"Why did Mads take that little girl?"

Ruslan glanced over at another customer, reading his phone. Cut his voice down. "Because she's one of them."

"And you brought her to the hospital to—"

"Deprogram her."

"I see."

The man nodded, leaned back. "You never know who might be one of them. It's early days—prototypes, but that's why we have to stop them now."

"And who is Mads and Alan hoping to stop."

Ruslan shrugged, both shoulders. "But it's someone important."

Right.

"Can I see the device?"

The man leaned back, shook his head. "No. Mads would be angry. And Alan..." He blew out another breath. "No."

"Okay. No problem." York held up his hands. Then, he held one out to Ruslan. "But if you ever need help, you can call me, okay?"

Ruslan considered his hand, then reached out and shook it.

Craziest moment York had ever experienced with an asset.

He scribbled the number to his burner phone on a napkin, and Ruslan wadded it in his pocket as he got up.

"Keep up the good fight," York said and held up his fist.

Ruslan bumped it, then threw his cup out on his way out the door.

York simply stood there, weaving through the conversation, giving Ruslan a few steps before he followed him.

Well, he'd heard crazier stories, right? Alien abductions. People returning from the dead—

Maybe that one wasn't so crazy.

But still, given the advancing technology, robotics, Alexa driven devices...okay, he could buy the psychosis.

Still, it gave him pause as to how much people could dream up their own terror. Their own demise.

Then he headed out into the street and turned in the direction of the end of the game.

Berlin, Germany

"Seriously? One phone call and you're on a plane across the

world to rescue me?" RJ stood, her hands on her hips, fire in her eyes, just a scuff of red on her chin the remainder of their collision.

In full disclosure, Tate didn't actually think RJ would be thrilled to see him.

After all, the idea of her brothers running to her aid, like she might be a ten-year-old who'd fallen off her horse always set her on her teeth.

But when Ziggy had motioned to him to find her last night, after hearing her voice through the comms, yeah, the charade was up, and he was all in, sprinting through the castle of the crazy king to the fifth—not the third—floor, up the circular stairs and—

He'd nearly taken her out. Managed to catch her and twist, landing first on the floor, cushioning her fall.

Mostly.

Because she hit pretty hard, he thought, given the sound she made. Or maybe that was just shock as she sat up and looked at him, the appropriate amount of disbelief on her face, and said, "What are you doing here?"

The shock still sort of remained in her expression even twenty-four hours later, as they stood in a hotel room in downtown Berlin, a stone's throw from the Brandenburg gates, their first real chance to talk after the fiasco at the castle.

"It might have been more than one call," he said now, in answer to her accusation.

"Perfect. What, did you have a family round table? No, wait, a *Zoom* call?"

He made a face.

"I was kidding. Oh my gosh!" She turned and walked to the window. Outside, the dusk fell across the street, hit the shiny windows, glared into the room. "I really can't believe you guys."

"I can't believe *you*." Maybe it was the fatigue of the past three days—getting on a plane in Nashville, flying to Berlin, renting a car, driving to Munich, meeting with Ziggy in private, his panic after hearing about her near-skydiving death—what was she thinking?—and then dodging her at the Awards ceremony, while also watching her back.

So yeah, he was crabby. And he didn't like to lie to his sister. But more— "Who do you think you are? 007? You nearly got yourself killed."

"Hardly. I got away—"

"You destroyed a hundred-year-old historical treasure! You're lucky you didn't have charges filed. And you could have killed one of Win's bodyguards!"

"Clearly, it was just a little misunderstanding."

"Declan thought you were going to assassinate Winchester Marshall. That isn't just *a little* misunderstanding."

"And I thought he might be the guy who destroyed our parachutes!"

Silence, because yes, that thought caught him up, and he heard the terror of it in her voice, fresh and raw.

"And I'm not the only one. Win was really mad—you saw him."

Yeah, he did, and that was after he'd won some big award. Ziggy had pulled him away from their front row seats into some side room after the castle security had dug out Declan, some on-site EMTs had splinted his ankle, and after Lake had told them the story of how he'd seen someone on the balcony.

"You guys should have told Lake and Declan what you were up to. Then Lake would have never sent him up there."

"After saving my life, you'd think Lake would have recognized me."

"I didn't see you, so maybe not. And Winchester certainly

didn't know you were there to spy on him. He nearly lost it. When did you become friends?"

It freaked him out a little the way Winchester had pulled her into his arms like they were family.

Okay, but—

She sighed. "Poor Declan." She turned, her arms folded. "How is he, by the way?"

"Busted ankle, and you broke his nose."

She made a face.

"Which I suppose should make me a little less freaked out, but seriously, RJ. You're in over your head."

She stared at him, her eyes widening. Then, "You think?"

He recoiled. Oh.

"My husband might be dead. Someone is trying to kill Winchester—or me—and you think that I'm not completely freaked out?"

So much to unpack. Starting with— "Your *husband?*"

Her mouth opened. Closed. She drew in a breath. "We got married a couple weeks ago."

"Married."

"Congratulations?"

"And you didn't think to tell any of us? Mom?"

"I called her. She knows."

And that made him feel a little slapped. Although, they'd left her out of the Zoom meeting so she wouldn't worry.

Maybe he'd—they'd—deserved that just a little.

"But none of your family was there."

"It was a spur of the moment decision." Sighing, she walked over to the sofa and sat. "There was a lot going on."

He sat on the coffee table in front of her. "I get that. I do. But family matters, RJ." He touched her hand. "You should have let us in, to help."

"To get lectured."

NO MATTER THE COST

Okay, maybe he deserved that. He pulled his hand away. "Sorry. It's just—we don't want anything to happen to you."

"That's not your job, Tate."

"It was."

Now she touched his hand. "I'm firing you."

He smiled, then. "You can fire me after we figure out what is going on."

She narrowed her eyes. "Okay, you're on probation. But no more sneaking around Europe without telling me."

"Deal." He got up, walked to the window. "So, let's go back to the other thing."

"What other thing?"

He turned. "York."

She looked away.

"Sis."

"I know you're going to call me crazy, but he's not dead—"

"I believe you—"

"Because last time, he wasn't dead, and we even had a body—"

"I believe you, RJ—"

"And I know I'd just feel it, you know? Deep inside—what?"

He came over and sat next to her on the sofa. "I believe you."

"You do?" And then her eyes filled. "You do."

"Mmmhmm." He put his arms around her and pulled her to his chest. "I should have believed you before, about Reba Jackson, and if you believe York is alive, I do too."

She turned quiet, and in his arms, her body began to shake.

"RJ?"

"Don't say anything. Don't look at me. I just need a moment here."

He smiled and pressed his cheek against her head. "It's going to be okay."

She drew in a long breath and made a sound. Maybe agreement.

"Now, the really big question."

She pulled away, wiped her cheeks. "Who tried to kill him?"

"Oh yeah, that. But I was thinking—were you really in a commercial with Winchester Marshall?"

She laughed, and it felt like sunshine in his soul. "Oh, Tate. I'm so glad you're here."

He didn't know why those words felt like forgiveness.

"I'm starved. How about I take you out for dinner and you tell me whether this guy is really our cousin. And of course, when your next big movie is out."

SEVEN

B erlin, Germany

Don't lose him. Don't get caught.

RJs voice, in York's head, and he probably deserved it because he'd said the exact words to her that terrible, fateful day when she'd gone after a man named Abu Massif and ignited this whole off-the-hook escapade.

Which, if he played his tail right, ducking in and out of the deepening shadows, keeping his eye on his quarry—Ruslan— every second, might be nearing a finale.

Ruslan wasn't even trying. He practically strolled, his satchel over his shoulder, working his phone as if he might be playing a game. He'd nearly run into a woman, a garbage can, a dog, and practically tripped off the sidewalk as the light turned red. Saved by a man in a business suit who'd righted him back onto the sidewalk before a truck took him out.

And that would have been tragic. Because Ruslan was York's only lead. His last lead. His best lead to what really might be going on.

He stuck his hands in his pockets, not making eye contact with the increasing foot traffic—men and women walking to the U-Bahn or the bus stop and ran his confusing conversation with Ruslan through his mind. *It keeps the voices from talking to me.*

Sometimes York would like to keep the voices from talking to *him.*

Okay, Ruslan's mental illness wasn't funny, and York shouldn't call him crazy. Poor man had let his fears take hold of him, cause him to do unthinkable crimes. So, he was to be pitied.

And stopped.

But it did make him think about the fact that he'd let his fear of the past grab hold so hard to a future he thought he wanted that it blinded him to the truth.

He was good at this. Or at least had been, and maybe he needed to pay attention to his own words. *"We can't save ourselves, even if we wanted to. That's the point of everything God does—to save us."*

It wasn't lost on him that somehow, despite the craziness, God had reached through the haze and led him to the truths of Claire and Lucas' deaths.

And then he'd helped him find Ruslan.

And maybe, frankly, he'd been guiding York for longer than he could remember, bringing him back to the man he'd wanted to be. Including erasing his memory, and giving him a new future and...

And maybe he should stop arranging for himself the life he thought he wanted and start trusting God for the life he wanted to give him.

NO MATTER THE COST

Them. Because RJ was so close—or at least the thought of her—he could nearly see her.

Dark hair, wearing a black sun dress, a pair of sandals, walking in front of him, some twenty paces before she disappeared into a building.

He glanced at it as he walked by, wishing. Ironically, it was his hotel, the one with the rooftop cafe.

Ruslan nearly disappeared in that space of time, and when York turned back, he saw the man halt, glance toward an alleyway between buildings, then step out of view.

He picked up his hustle.

No, not an alleyway—an underground parking garage. Maybe this was where Ruslan accessed his flat—or wherever he'd been holding up while he worked on Nika.

Darkness, and a cool breath licked over him as he entered, slowed, his eyes on an exit, but the ramp led him down into a small dimly lit area.

A shout echoed, a scream of panic squelched. It raised the skin on the back of his neck and York took off toward it, heart thumping.

A fist in his gut.

He spotted first the puddle of blood, fresh, red, pooling out onto the concrete about half-way down the aisle, then Ruslan's body, crumpled between a Mercedes and a BMW, lifeless, his satchel ripped from his body.

Oh. *No.*

York nearly lunged for him, hoping to save him, but a sound at the end of the aisle jerked his attention.

He glimpsed, in a flash of quick light, a man opening a door, and escaping through it.

Aw—

He took off, full run toward the door, yanked it open and found stairs.

Footsteps pounded above.

York took off, taking them two at a time, then slower as he reached the third floor.

A door closed above him.

He scrambled up, yanked open the door and saw a man on the far end of the hallway, running hard.

He held Ruslan's satchel in his hand.

York nearly let out a useless, Stop! But why? Instead, he lit out down the hallway, grateful that nearly three weeks had passed since he'd been stabbed. Still, the effort burned, deep inside.

But he wasn't losing his last, his only lead. Again.

The man rounded the end of the hallway, and York had caught up, almost forty feet behind him.

Not enough to stop him from going through the emergency exit, another set of stairs, this time, outside the building.

A fire escape.

The man was already two stories up and climbing hard.

York had maybe gained a step, or two, but not much when the man landed on the roof.

And disappeared.

He was really starting to hurt, his knife wounds and various other injuries protesting, but he hurtled over the top of the fire escape, to the edge of the roof, his feet landing on the tar and gravel. He found the man just vanishing behind a huge mechanical box.

The sun burned against the metal, red, gold, glaring in his eyes and he nearly fell as his feet skidded on the gravel.

He rounded the box, running hard. And his heart just about leaped from his body when he spotted the man taking a running leap—

Right off the building.

What—?

York ran to the end, catching himself and looked over.

The man had landed, twenty feet down, rolling onto the lower roof. The satchel lay a few feet away. He'd been injured, it seemed, because he roared, then grabbed his ankle.

Then he looked up.

And York's breath left his body.

Alan Martin. Yep, that was his old nemesis from Russia, the man who'd turned traitor, conjured up a plan to assassinate the president, and now was involved in some crazy, complicated plot to...do what?

York turned, backed up, turned again and ran hard.

Found air, his arms windmilling.

He landed hard, rolled, like he'd learned in the military, after a parachute landing, and came up on his feet.

Martin was already back up, running toward the satchel.

York leaped at him. Caught his collar and yanked him back.

Martin fell back, and York jumped ahead, his eye on the satchel.

A fist to his lower back, right in his healing wound sucked out his breath, buckled his knees.

But as he fell, he grabbed the satchel. He felt a tug, heard a curse, and then Martin was running again.

Oh no you don't.

York scrabbled to his feet, flung the satchel over his shoulder and took off.

Martin was limping, but clearly had decided to grit out the pain, and straightened out his run. The buildings here were connected and he hurtled the edge of one, landed, stumbled, then kept going.

But York was catching up.

He kept his gaze on Martin, on the way the man was straining, and the ground he was eating up and suddenly, he was...nearly...

He grabbed Martin's jacket, near the collar, and jerked. "Gotcha!"

Martin stumbled, fell back. Then, he simply peeled out of the jacket. Turned.

Threw his fist into York's face.

He took the hit. Threw down the jacket. Face the man. Martin was bleeding from a scrape on his jaw—probably from the fall—sweating and wore death on his face.

York tackled him. Martin went down, swearing, but boxed York hard, right in the back, on his healing wound.

He bit back a howl, leaned up and hit Martin.

Martin brought up his knee, and the world exploded, everything turning white with pain.

York rolled off, stifling another howl, fighting for breath.

Dirty—

Martin scrambled to his feet. "You should have stayed dead." He reached for the satchel, but York slapped away his hand.

"Hey! Everything okay over there?"

The voice from somewhere nearby lifted Martin's head. For a second, he seemed to debate. Then he took off, running hard for the next rooftop.

York forced himself to his feet, the world still searing around the edges and made himself follow him.

His last...lead....

He found himself just as he took the leap onto the next roof, Martin still in his sights, and only when he landed, did he realize he nearly took out a table. And a waiter.

And a tray of shrimp, and a planter and suddenly he was scampering through a rooftop cafe, on the trail of overturned tables and angry waiters and patrons with food on their laps—

Martin reached the stairs of the restaurant. Glanced back. Smiled.

Then he took off.

York leaped a table, dodged a waiter and was just about to the stairs—

"York!"

"So York really tried to drown the guy?"

Tate sat across from her at the Paris Hotel, the fancy five-star hotel Winchester had booked them in and for a long while, escaped the hold of grief.

Or maybe despair.

Still, the darkness that stalked her since she'd seen York fall —leap?—off a cliff seemed to lift with Tate's teasing, his laughter, or amazement at the story of her epic woes in Europe. Maybe it was just being with her brother—and the fact that he believed her. Or it could be the gorgeous sunset, the way the sky turned a mottled-orange and purple, the skyline of Berlin, and even St. Hedwig's cathedral with its massive green domed roof.

York would have loved this place.

But she let that thought spiral out of her and focused instead on the telling of how she'd met Winchester Marshall, and his odd tangle into their lives. "Well, he did steal York's reservation at the restaurant he wanted to propose at in Paris."

"Yikes."

"I know. And it was sort of Win's fault that all this started. He bumped into me in line at a coffee shop the next day, causing a cascade of disasters and got us ousted. He walked me to a different coffee shop, and it was there I spotted Alan Martin."

Tate frowned. "That's very coincidental."

"York said the same thing. So when he saw him in Italy, he just couldn't control himself. He just took the guy out into the pool. Pretty tough for a guy who'd gotten stabbed just a week before."

Tate was mid-drink and now put his infused water down. "What? York was stabbed?"

"That was after he drove a boat into this yacht that Alan Martin was on. He was trying to take out a plane, and York made it explode."

Tate wasn't moving.

"But we were okay," she said, leaning forward. "I'd gotten off the yacht by myself, and then Roy was there, so I was fine."

"Roy?"

Right. "Sorry. Roy was the guy who helped take down, um—"

"My mother-in-law."

"Yeah. Sorry. He works with us in the Caleb Group."

And she'd just said too much. It wasn't a secret, really, but given Tate's expression. "Okay, so we haven't caught up in a while."

"What is the Caleb Group?"

"It's sort of a private operations group put together by President White to hunt down terrorist operations—"

"Like the Petrov Bratva."

"You know about them?"

"I've been doing my own digging since..." He made a face. "Well, it's not like Glo and I have anywhere to go, or anything to do, really. Too much paparazzi, especially during the trial."

"Sorry."

"No. It's not your fault. It's mine. I should have...well, I already said it, but I should have listened to you. Believed you about Jackson."

"I understand, Tate. I mean, of course you had to support Glo. How is she?"

"Better. Started writing songs again. It's a good thing."

"And you?"

He shrugged. "I'm here. It's better than mowing the lawn."

She frowned. "Mowing—?"

"Forget it. Tell me why you think—why you know—York is still alive."

"Right. So how much do you know about the contract on York?"

"Coco brought me up to speed. Gutsy move, trying to see who paid out the contract."

"Or just a big fail. I nearly got trampled in a rush to the stage to see..." She paused. "Don't freak out."

"Don't—"

"Win was there."

Tate cocked his head. "He was at the bar where the payment for York's hit was going down?" He took a breath. "Okay, now I'm starting to agree with York."

"I know. Me too. Which was why I searched his hotel room."

"You did what? Please tell me you weren't caught."

"Oh no, I was. But that's the thing. Win covered for me. So, it can't be him."

Tate just blinked at her. "He's an actor, RJ. And, can I just mention his specialty is spy movies. Of course he covered for you." He leaned back, a hand behind his neck. Looked away.

"Tate, really. I trust him. There's just...something about him."

"Yeah. That he's handsome, and a movie star—"

"And our cousin!"

Tate frowned at that. "Second cousin. I looked him up. His dad was dad's cousin."

"So. Family then."

"It doesn't make him innocent."

"It does if someone tried to kill him."

"Or you. Maybe—"

"You didn't see him, Tate. He was completely rattled. Scared. No, he didn't sabotage his own chutes. I know it in my gut."

His mouth formed a tight line.

"Same gut that said Reba was guilty."

He took a breath. "Okay."

"But it doesn't mean that we don't watch him."

He frowned.

"There's something not right here. Because York's right—there are too many coincidences, too many happenstance meetings. It's like...we were supposed to see Alan Martin. Or maybe Alan was supposed to be there the same time Win was. Whatever...there's something. I can feel it."

"Can you feel your way to an appetizer?" He gestured to the waiter as he came over.

Tate leaned back, his arms folded across his chest. Despite his year of self-imposed house arrest, he looked good. Tan, his body lean and trim, as if he still worked out. Blondish-brown hair cut short, that slightly lopsided, troublemaker smile.

Yeah, she missed him. Missed all of her brothers, honestly.

Maybe it didn't hurt so much to be the little sister.

"Shrimp cocktail," she said, pointing to it on the menu.

"Nothing German?" Tate asked.

"I'm so tired of Schnitzel and bratwurst—no, I'm ready for something sort of normal."

"Then shrimp it is," he said.

The waiter left and Tate ran his finger down his glass. "I'm ready for something normal too. Except my normal is to do something...I don't know—meaningful? With my life. I can't sit around the house anymore hoping that I get a phone call where my sister needs me."

She smiled. "Who called you anyway?"

"Coco called Glo. But Ziggy called Coco. And then, eventually, I got ahold of Ziggy."

"And ended up nearly killing me."

He made a face. "Oops."

"So, back to normal, then."

He laughed, and his smile hit his eyes. "Touché."

She laughed too. "Don't worry, Tate. I know something will happen. Just wait—it's probably right around—"

A shout down at the end of the cafe lifted. A waiter, looking over the rooftop to the next one.

Tate also turned around.

But RJ froze. Because just then, a man appeared, jumping off the edge of the roof.

He took down the waiter, stumbled, then ran down the center of the restaurant, pushing waiters, turning over a table, two, as if to clutter the path behind him.

Tate got up, rounded the table and pulled RJ up, and out of the way.

"What's going on?"

"I don't know."

She spotted their waiter and wanted to warn him because his back was to the man—

The shrimp went flying. The waiter hit the ground and RJ pressed her hand to her mouth to ward off a scream.

Because that's when she saw him. Tall, dark hair, a scar across his forehead.

Alan Martin.

Running straight for her.

She didn't know if he'd seen her or not, but she picked up a butter knife from the table.

"What are you doing?" Tate grabbed her back just as Martin ran by.

"That's him—that's Martin!"

As if he heard his name, he turned just as he hit the stairwell.

For a second, his gaze fell on her, then he blinked, and it swept past her, toward the mess behind him.

And he smiled.

What—?

She turned to see what—

And then she froze.Her breath turned to ice inside her.

Because on his tail, leaping tables, and pushing past waiters and even slipping on shrimp was—

Oh. She put her hand to her chest, still unable to breathe.

He had dark hair and a beard, ripped pants, a dirty suit coat and wore such an intense expression of pursuit on his face, she just knew—

He was going after Alan Martin.

And she might never see him again.

No. Not again.

Not ever again.

He passed her, didn't even look at her, his gaze pinned on Martin, who'd vanished down the stairs.

And that's when she found her voice. With everything inside her, she let it out, praying he heard it through his haze of fury.

"*York!*"

He stopped, catching himself on the edge of the stairwell, his hand on the railing. Whirled around.

She couldn't move.

He was alive—she always knew it—but to see him standing there, brutal, tough, intense—the man she'd met years ago, the man he still was—the reality of it simply swept through her.

York.

Then he looked down the stairs, as if he might follow Martin.

Everything inside her started to shatter. *Please—*

Then, just like that he turned away, toward her, and advanced. He stepped over a fallen chair, pushed past a waiter, standing there watching, walked around a table, and his expression was so solemn, so resolute, she barely caught a breath before he was in front of her.

Her eyes widened. Then he simply put his hand around the back of her neck, and kissed her.

The kind of kiss that told her everything she already knew.

She was his, and he was hers and nothing, not even death, could keep him from coming back to her.

She grabbed his suit coat lapels and hung on.

York.

He finally let her go, leaning back. Took a breath.

"You'll find him again," she said quietly. "*We'll* find him again."

He considered her a moment, then smiled. "Yes. Yes we will." He lifted the satchel. "This belonged to Ruslan Gustov. And you won't believe the story I have to tell."

She took his hands. "Right back atcha."

CHAPTER
EIGHT

Berlin, Germany

He'd nearly kept running.

The thought spiked through York again—too many times, really—over the past hour as he and Tate and the waiters helped pick up tables, clean up shrimp and finally apologize to the manager for the destruction Martin—and he—had wrought.

If only that destruction ended with some broken glasses and wasted food.

"You know, RJ never believed you were dead."

This from Tate. It had taken York a full minute to get his head around the fact that his brother-in-law was standing with RJ on the roof. And for his part, Tate appeared undone by York's appearance. "Who are you?" he'd said. "Batman?"

York had let himself grin at that even as Tate took his hand, then pulled him in for a slap.

"Tired," York had answered, to which Tate also laughed.

"You look it, man."

Amazingly, the manager hadn't kicked them out, but let them finish dinner on the rooftop as the night descended, stars appearing to shine upon them, the sweet fragrance of uncorked wine, grilled steak, the scent of roses stirred up by a slight, perfect breeze.

Yeah, he'd nearly kept running, and sure he might have caught Martin.

Or he might have been killed. And never been reunited with his wife.

Now, he wove his fingers through RJ's under the table. He'd cleaned up, a little, in the bathroom, put a wet towel to the scrape on his jaw, but his beard hid it well. Wiped off his clothing. Tried to wipe from his face the fatigue of the last two weeks.

Then he'd opened the satchel. Inside he found the money Alan had killed for, along with a key, Ruslan's meds, and a couple girlie magazines. Unfortunately, no map, or written private journal of Martin's nefarious activities.

York was getting a little giddy, clearly.

Meanwhile, RJ had called Ziggy to inform her of Ruslan's death in the garage and give her the quiet news of his return. Ziggy would call the right authorities and tip them off about Ruslan, hopefully keeping them all out of it.

"I didn't think she would," York said. He glanced at her.

If possible, she was even more beautiful than the last time he saw her—although then, she'd been dressed in a ball gown, her dark hair curled, her blue eyes caught in his, trusting, believing. His partner.

A few seconds later, she'd pointed out a man who bore the tattoo of the Orphans.

But tonight, she also wore the look of confidence.

"But admittedly, you went over the cliff, bro. How did you survive?"

Tate looked good, although York hadn't seen him since the night they'd arrested Jackson. Even last Christmas, he and Glo hadn't come home, not wanting to drag the press to the Marshall ranch in Montana. And when Tate told him the story of Ziggy's call to Coco and how it landed him across the ocean, York could admit to a hint of relief that indeed, her brothers still had her back.

Not that she couldn't take care of herself, but...well, he knew his wife.

Wife. He looked at her and squeezed her hand. Oh, yes. He'd made the right decision. And they would find Martin again.

Together.

"We landed in the water— me on top of him. He took the brunt of the force, but I was jarred off him. The water took me out and I couldn't get back. A fishing trawler picked me up, and it was then I doubled down on the plan that if I was dead, then maybe we could find out who placed the hit on me when he paid the Orphans."

"I tried that," RJ said. "Coco and I tracked down Raisa Yaka-chova and I followed her to a bar in—"

"Prague. I know. You wore red hair. And a dress that should be illegal."

Her mouth opened. "I did see you!"

"Mmmhmm."

She closed her mouth, shook her head. "I knew it."

"You have good instincts."

"Ziggy thought she saw you too, but you disappeared before she could follow you."

He ignored an explanation. "I was following Raisa."

"Did you catch her?"

"Yeah."

RJ's eyes widened. "And—did you find out who put the hit on you?"

"No." He glanced at Tate.

"He knows everything," RJ said, as if in confirmation of his unspoken question about Tate's need to know.

"Okay. The night we were playing decoy for Landon Grey, the CDC director, even though I had a contract on me, the Orphan was there for Grey. I was just the bonus round. Yes, Raisa was collecting for my bounty, but since it was paid, the contract was retired, the contract and its details deleted. The only thing she still had was the contract on Landon. Which, by the way, was canceled."

"You got nothing?" Tate said. The waiter had stopped by, refilled their glasses of infused water and served them a plate of fresh shrimp. Tate picked one up and dipped it into the cold cocktail sauce.

"Not exactly. She was able to track the money to an old Russian contact we had, a Bratva accountant named Pasha."

"So the Bratva put a hit out on Grey?"

"No. Pasha was skimming money from them, paying it out to Ruslan Gustov."

"Ruslan? Are you sure?"

"I was. I even thought that maybe he'd taken out the contract on me, too. But then, I tracked down Ruslan." He considered the shrimp, but the pretzel still sat in his stomach, despite the adrenaline of the past two hours.

Instead, he looked at RJ. "Ruslan is...he's suffers from a mental illness."

She just stared at him.

"He thinks we're going to be invaded by Skynet."

A beat.

"As in *The Terminator*?" Tate said softly. "What?"

"Yes. He's on meds to stop the voices in his head. And he told me how the Marx device—which he calls Nika—is supposed to save the world from AI."

More silence. RJ just looked at him, frowning. "You're serious."

"As a boy scout."

"He tried to blow up a plane! And he kidnapped me!"

"He said the plane was full of AIs. That he was trying to stop them—I think Alan Martin was playing with his head."

"That's—"

"I'm telling you, RJ—he was unhinged. Even after he took his meds."

She reached out for a shrimp. "Could be mental illness runs in the family. After all, I'd call his brother Damien just a little obsessed."

"Clearly Martin was using him for his science. And Mads— who, by the way, took Hana from an orphanage where Pasha had hidden her."

"Pasha?"

"Her grandfather. The Bratva accountant. And a former asset."

"Your asset," Tate said.

"A long time ago. His daughter was murdered, and Pasha panicked and put Hana—real name Ania—in an orphanage to protect her."

"Like Coco with Mikka," RJ said.

He nodded. "Pasha was crazy with grief, not knowing what happened to her. I told him Hana was safe, and he didn't want to know where."

"Plausible deniability," Tate said, wiping his fingers on a napkin.

"That's so sad."

"Is it?" York said. "She's safe, and away from the Bratva. I think that's a win. And my guess is that Pasha does too."

She nodded. "What will happen to her?"

York had landed on something during his plane ride from Russia, but it felt a little too young and tender to voice, so, "Not sure yet. I have some ideas."

RJ sighed, finished eating her shrimp.

"What I'd like to know is what is Alan Martin up to, and how did he get free?" Tate said.

"Not sure about that," York said, "You'd have to talk to Logan Thorne for those details."

"He's in charge of the Caleb Group?"

York blinked at him, then looked at RJ. "He knows everything?"

"Yes." She smiled. "Everything."

Oh. He glanced at Tate, who was grinning at him. "Congrats, bro. Welcome to the fam." He lifted his water glass.

York didn't know what he expected, but the warmth that filled him caught him off guard. "Thanks."

"So, don't make my sister a widow again, okay?"

York nodded, his gaze turning to RJ. "Never again."

She cocked her head at him. "Oh, York. Never say never. It's like a dare to all the cosmic forces of evil."

He laughed, and everything suddenly broke open—the past two weeks of panic and despair and desperation. She grinned too, her blue eyes shining.

They could probably ditch dinner. After all, they were supposed to be on their honeymoon.

The waiter came by, however, and delivered their order. A lambchop for him, pasta for RJ, a steak for Tate.

Suddenly, York was ravenous. He dug in. "So, after I saw you in Prague what happened?"

She twirled her fork into her pasta—seafood in creamy Alfredo sauce.

"You mean after Win rescued me from being trampled?" She rolled the pasta onto a spoon. Looked at him.

Oh. Right. "For your information, I was on my way down the stairs when he scooped you up. I wouldn't have let you get trampled to death."

She looked at him, an emotion in her eyes he couldn't place. "I know."

And the words sort of exploded in him. See, this was what being married was all about—partnership. Trust. One epic day at a time, even when they didn't see the future.

He smiled back. Then, "Did you not think it strange that Win showed up again? Right where you never expected him to be?"

"Of course I did." She finished chewing, wiped her mouth. "Which is why I went with him back to his hotel room and searched his room."

"Searched—"

"Calm down, bud," Tate said. "I already did this part. Lake caught her. Win covered for her—"

"He's an actor!"

"Yep. Said that part too—"

"I believe him," RJ said, sliding her hand onto York's arm.

"Tell him about the payment, RJ." Tate said, cutting into his steak. He raised an eyebrow at York.

"What payment?" York growled.

"Calm down. We're tracking it down. Win had a half-mil stolen from his account two days before the payment for your contract went down."

His appetite died and he pushed his plate away. "*What*—?"

He looked at Tate who nodded grimly. "Winchester Marshall paid for the contract on my life."

He knew it. *Knew* it. But why?

"Win had no idea," RJ said. "He even gave me his computer to use to track down the transfer. Coco and I are on it, but..." She shook her head. "York. Someone tried to kill Win a few days later. If he did it, why is he a target?"

"She forgot to mention that she was strapped to Win during said murder attempt."

York just stared at Tate. *"What?"*

"Tate." RJ gave him a look of annoyance. Turned to York. "We were skydiving. Tandem. Win's a certified jumper. But someone had tangled his primary chute and cut the canopy on his secondary so—"

"Are you kidding me?"

"Breathe, babe."

He might never breathe again.

"Lake rescued me—he caught up to me in free-fall, sort of hooked me to him, and deployed his chute for both of us. And the tandem master did the same for Win." She pushed her plate away. "So, you see, Win is not trying to kill me. Or you."

"Well, I was already dead, so..." He looked away, into the night. The stars blinked down at him, seeing what he couldn't.

Lord...

He didn't know why his brain, his thoughts immediately reached upward, but frankly, that wasn't a bad idea.

He might be blind, but God saw the whole picture.

York sighed, nodded. "So, someone on Win's team stole his money, used it to pay for my contract, and then tried to kill Win—or both of you." He turned back to her. "So, what happens when said person finds out I'm still alive?"

"I say we find out," Tate said quietly. Then smiled.

York looked at him and smiled back.

But RJ touched York's cheek, ran her thumb through his beard. "But not quite yet. York and I need a minute to ourselves."

He looked into her blue eyes, the memories stirring inside and nodded.

She never wanted to leave this room.

Not with her man—her husband—tangled in the sheets next to her, laying on his stomach, his head in his pillow, cradled in his arms. He was sleeping like the dead—so soundly, actually, that she'd put her hand on his back once in the night just to confirm—and it only told her just how tightly wound, exhausted and frenetic he'd been to track down his killer over the past two weeks.

His killer, and whatever plan Martin was hatching.

And no small part of that was trying to keep her safe, of course.

She'd felt his relief last night, after they'd gotten to her hotel room, when he'd kicked shut her door, grabbed her, spun her back to him, then pressed her against the wall and kissed her.

The kind of kiss that spectators shouldn't watch.

But the kiss that told her that he'd had every intention of returning to her.

He'd finally released her—and frankly, she'd fought it—and pressed his forehead to hers. "I told you I'd be right back."

And then she laughed with the absurdity of it all, and because indeed, he'd said that, just like she'd said the same words to him, and because yes, he was most definitely alive, and whole and maybe something was different, either, because in his touch, in his kiss, she felt the man she met years ago.

Confident. Dangerous. Passionate. Intense.

And she was his entire focus.

At least she had been for the better part of the night.

She rolled over to her side, touching his beard. Such a strange look, but she didn't hate it. It reminded her a little of the man he'd been back in Shelly. No secrets, just his heart, wanting to be a good man.

And just like that she got it. His desire to return to that safe, quiet life.

Because there, he could forget the past. Be Mack, the grill master.

But that wasn't honest, was it? Because York would always have this other part, the Bird, the man who just couldn't stop himself from *getting involved*.

And maybe that's what she'd wanted. Not just to do something that mattered, but to do it with *him*.

He stirred, and she removed her hand, but he opened his eyes. So blue, and in a moment, focused on her. He smiled. "Hey there, Syd."

Heat poured through her as she met his eyes, her head on her pillow. Especially when his gaze went to her lips.

He leaned over and kissed her, gently, then pulled away. "You were thinking." He settled his head on his pillow again. "What about?"

"What if we already have our happy ending?"

He raised an eyebrow.

"I know I've spent all this time wanting more. To be more. That I wanted to train at the farm, and do all these spectacular things, but maybe...I think I just wanted to be as amazing as you. To be in your world. See it through your eyes."

"You don't want to see what I see, babe."

"Maybe not. But..." She pressed her hands together under her cheek. "Even Sydney had to retire."

"You forget what Sydney's father said to her, though," York said

She looked at him. "You watched Alias?"

"It's a little crazy—"

She kissed him. He caught her around the neck, held her there.

She finally pulled away.

"What was that for?"

"For caring about the world in my head."

"Babe. I always care about the world in your head."

"Even if it gets us into trouble."

"Trouble will always be out there. We can't live in fear of it. Or trying to hide from it. That was my mistake."

Her eyes widened. "Really?"

He propped himself up on one arm, his head on his hand. "Sydney's father told her that while he never wanted the clandestine life for her, there was no one who could do what she did." He reached out and tucked an errant strand of hair behind her ear. "The last two weeks has taught me that maybe I need to stop worrying so hard about creating the safe life I want to live and realize that God can sort this for us. I just have to live today, trusting. Being. Saying yes."

"To what?"

"To you. To the life God wants to give us."

"But what if we don't know what that is?"

He wrapped an arm around her waist, pulling her close to him, tucking the covers around her shoulders. "Then we wait until he shows us."

Yes. Because of course God showed up to answer her prayers on the roof of a building, a high tower.

"And until then..." He bent his head and kissed her.

Oh yes. She could get on board with waiting.

The sun slipped into the room, fingers of rose gold upon the bedsheets when York finally got up, went to the bathroom and turned on the shower. RJ curled into the sheets, her thoughts upon the day.

"What if we don't leave?"

He poked his head out of the room. "Yes."

She laughed and got up, pulling the sheet around her. Went to stand at the window. The morning glinted against the windows of the buildings, the green cathedral, even the cobblestone square some five stories below. "So, what's on our itinerary today?"

No answer. He'd probably gotten into the shower. She went to the coffee pot on the bureau and grabbed the pot. Filled it with bottled water.

Watched the coffee drip, staring at it.

They still hadn't figured out who was after Grey. Or who wanted York dead. Or how Win was involved—because she agreed with York. He had to be involved. Or how, even she'd ended up on a rooftop cafe that was directly in line with Martin's getaway plan.

Except...

Why had Win booked them at *this* hotel?

"I love a wife who can make coffee." York came out of the bathroom, his hair tousled and wet, wearing just a towel around his lean hips. He wore a scattering of bruises across his body, ones she hadn't seen in last night's dim light. She must have betrayed her horror because he came up to her, caught her face in his hands. "I'm fine."

Then he kissed her, and she nearly dragged him back to the tangled sheets.

Instead, she pushed on his amazing chest, met his eyes. "Why did Win book us here?"

145

SUSAN MAY WARREN

He stepped up, put his arm around her waist. "Because it's a five-star hotel?" He kissed her neck.

Maybe it didn't matter. She went to put her arms around him.

He raised his head. "But, good question because I'm also booked here."

She met his eyes. "Now you tell me?"

"I wasn't thinking about details last night."

"So you're here. I'm here. Win's here..."

His mouth tightened. "Who else is here? Why did he come to Berlin?"

"I don't know. He was pretty shaken after the event in Neuschwanstein castle. Lake pretty much took charge after Declan was hospitalized. I think he made the arrangements. Or maybe this was the plan all along. He mentioned some publicity event, but I thought that was the Arts in Film award show. Maybe he meant something different. All I know is that one minute I was covered in rubble, the next we were on Win's plane to Berlin."

He nodded, walked to the window. "From here I can see the cathedral. The University. The Humboldt Forum."

She poured herself a cup of coffee, another for him. Came to join him. Stared at the stately Humboldt Forum building, something pinging inside her.

"Grey said he was coming here after Lauchtenland. An international symposium on viruses, or something like that." She leaned past him. "It looks like there are barriers around the doorways of the Forum. And, guards."

"I wonder if that's where it's being held," York said.

She stepped back, still trailing her sheet, and sat on the edge of the bed. "Remember what Coco said about Ruslan having the itinerary of the Russian general Stanislov? And Grey?"

146

York turned. "You don't think we're back there, do you?"

"The scenario where we walk into another assassination attempt on a Russian general? Oh, I hope not."

He leaned against the wall. "Why not. Relive old times..."

"Thanks, but I don't want to run for my life on my honeymoon."

"We do need a honeymoon." He smiled at her.

"Don't touch that towel, bub. And not a step closer. I need to think." She got up. "Maybe it's just a coincidence."

"Nothing is a coincidence."

She sighed. "Right. I need a shower." She shuffled to the bathroom, her train behind her, and shut the door. Locked it.

"I heard that!"

"Get dressed, Casanova."

But she smiled as she spotted herself in the mirror. Hair tousled, her face flushed. Happy.

Whole.

Yes, all she needed was York. Wherever they were.

Thank you, Lord, for this view.

She stepped into the shower.

Ten minutes later she stepped out of the bathroom, the bathrobe knotted around her, her hair damp.

To an empty room.

"York?"

It wasn't such a big room that he'd get lost. Weird.

She found a dress in her ever-changing wardrobe, and a pair of sandals and was in the bathroom drying her hair when the door opened.

York walked in carrying a backpack, in a fresh pair of jeans, shoes, and a clean white dress shirt, the cuffs rolled up. And, he'd shaved.

Oh. Sad.

But he smelled amazing. "Hey there, vagabond."

"I'm moving in." He dropped the backpack on the bed. "And I grabbed a paper from the lobby." He sat down, folded it open.

A USA Today, in English. He picked up his coffee and opened the paper.

She felt like an old-married couple.

Kathryn's makeup gal had given her a few supplies, so she put on some mascara and lipstick and came out of the bathroom, her hair still damp.

But ready for whatever he— "What?"

York had set the paper in his lap, was staring out the window, holding his coffee cup. At her question, he looked at her. Blinked.

"President White is here. For the symposium."

RJ sank onto the bed. A beat landed between them, as York took a breath. And then RJ voiced it for both of them. "It can't be that simple, can it?"

"It *is* Alan Martin," York said, very quietly. "And he seems to have one agenda."

RJ took a breath. Shook her head. "He's going to try and kill the president of the United States."

York just stared at her, his mouth tight.

Then he got up. Folded the paper and set it back on the chair.

Held out his hand.

"What's going on?"

"We're going to go talk to your friend Jack Powers."

"Oh, York. Please—behave yourself."

He looked at her. Kissed her cheek as he opened the door. Smiled. "Better hope there's not a pool nearby."

Then he winked and pulled her out the door.

CHAPTER
NINE

Berlin, Germany

Good thing the pool was six stories down because York didn't know what to make of Win's story.

Even though it jived with RJ's account, everything from the missing money to the skydiving accident.

Maybe because Win didn't seem that surprised to see York, alive.

"York!" Win had risen from his breakfast table where he sat with Tate Marshall. "You're a sight for sore eyes."

Sheesh, York wanted to believe Win. He was all smiles, and handshakes and a thump on the back like they might be long-lost war buddies. "RJ knew you weren't dead, of course." Win smiled over at RJ like they were besties.

RJ slipped her hand into York's, squeezed.

Tate had risen from the table, too, and York noted he wore

a pair of suit pants, a dress shirt, a jacket, his chin clean shaven.

Like he might be interviewing for a job?

York greeted him, then turned to Win. "We need to talk."

Win gestured to the table, and York let RJ around to the far side, pulled out her chair, then sat next to her.

"Fruit?" Win said and picked up a bowl from the table.

"I'd prefer answers."

Win had set the bowl down, taken a breath, and then folded his hands. "Fire away."

So, he had, asking about the payment, what he knew about the accident, even asking about the people who had access to his account.

"Just Brielle, my personal assistant. And my accountant, but she only had limited access. She couldn't withdraw funds. But she died before the money was transferred."

Same information RJ had given him, but like his wife, York couldn't dodge the sense that Win was telling the truth. Despite his status as an actor.

A knock came at the door about then and Lake got up to answer it. "Special services are here, sir, for your suit."

"It's hanging in my room," Win said. He turned to RJ and York. "Had a little mishap with some German chocolate cake and a waiter last night at the event I attended. The hotel is picking up my cleaning tab."

"What event was that?" RJ asked as Lake retrieved the suit and delivered it to the door.

"A charity event in conjunction with the World Symposium on Health Regulations. It's a global support organization that raises money for the health care of the impoverished in third world countries."

"Your publicity event," RJ said.

"My PR company set it up, so I assumed it would be about

the cameras. But actually, the event was private, and apparently, they want me to consider being an international spokesperson."

York didn't know what to make of that, except, maybe it was a good way for a wanna-be spy to use his skills.

He set his inner alert down to DEFCON five.

"Besides, it gave me a chance to catch up with Isaac."

York stilled. "Isaac—?"

"Sorry. President White. I know I should get used to that, but we were friends before he was in politics, so I have to keep assigning his titles to him. Feels strange." Win lifted a shoulder.

He looked at RJ who seemed not jarred at all by this news.

"You and the president are friends?" Tate said, with appropriate amount of surprise in his voice.

"Yes." He frowned. "He actually is using one of my houses for some surveillance he's doing with his private security group."

And York simply had...nothing. "The Caleb Group."

"That's the one. I told him he could use it anytime, and apparently, he took me up on the offer."

York looked at RJ. Back to Win. "You know we're a part of that group."

His mouth opened. He looked at RJ. "So that's what you were talking about."

Again, RJ just nodded.

Oh boy. But he'd get to the bottom of all the conversations he'd missed later. "We need to talk to the president."

He could call Logan, and set it up—that was going to be his next move. But—

"Sure. I'll text him and see if he's available." Win picked up his cell phone.

"You'll...just *text* him?"

"Well, his chief of staff, but I'll CC him on the text, yes." Win typed in the request to the silence of both Tate and York.

RJ reached for an orange and started to peel it with a spoon.

"Done." Win set the phone down. "Why by the way?"

"I think he's in danger," York said, not sure how much to tell Win.

"He's always in danger, right?" He looked at Tate, who nodded, his face grim. Win leaned forward, and reached out, his hand on Tate's shoulder. "It's not your fault."

Tate just looked at him.

Win removed his hand. "Okay, well, I'm going to get changed—"

The phone buzzed. Win picked it up. "He says he'll meet us in his suite in an hour." He got up. "I'm going to take a shower. I'll meet you guys in the lobby."

York couldn't help but feel summarily dismissed. "I guess we'll go find some breakfast."

Lake closed the door behind them as he, Tate and RJ left.

"Did that feel weird to you?" York said, in the hallway.

"That Winchester knows President White?" Tate asked.

"Mmmhmm."

"I don't know." Tate pressed the elevator button. "I don't know what to think." The elevator arrived and they got in. "The whole thing feels like a terribly small world. First, I can't believe he's really our cousin."

RJ had just put an orange slice in her mouth, and now nodded.

"And he just offered me a job. Apparently, Declan has resigned."

York looked at RJ. "Do you still suspect him?"

"I don't know. Coco did a background check on him—he's a former marine. Seems solid. No money issues."

The doors opened to the lobby and York led them to a coffee area. He poured cups for himself and RJ, and Tate grabbed one also, and they sat in the leather chairs under the glittering gold lights. Around them, people of all nationalities wandered the lobby, some of them checking out, others waiting in line for the restaurant.

RJ nodded to a couple of men in suits at the door. "Is the president staying *here*?"

York scanned the room. Spotted security at the coffee bar, seated in a chair, by the door—yes—and even a woman reading a paper wearing an earwig. "My guess is yes."

RJ looked at him. "You think Win chose this hotel because he knew where the president was staying?"

And now he was back at DEFCON three. Maybe two.

"Didn't you say that Lake recommended it?" York said now.

RJ had finished her orange, and now cupped her coffee with both hands. "I can't remember." She put her cup down. "But I'll ask Coco."

"It's midnight in Seattle," Tate said.

RJ gave him a look.

"Right," Tate said.

While RJ tapped out a text to her sister, the elevator doors opened, and Lake walked out. Went up to the concierge. Asked a question. The concierge looked up something in his computer, then wrote something down on a card and handed it to Lake. He shook the man's hand and headed back to the elevators.

"I'll be right back." York walked over to the concierge. An older gentleman, he wore a suit, a nametag. "Guten Morgen, Franz." York held out his hand. "I'm with Lake, Mr. Marshall's private security and I was wondering what time Mr. Marshall's car will be here."

Franz frowned. "Mr. Gunther didn't order a car, sir. Just pick up of Mr. Marshall's luggage for the airport."

"Right. Okay, maybe he's still waiting on the order for the car. Thank you." He walked back to the group. "He is transporting Win's luggage to the airport."

"Are we leaving?" RJ said.

Tate nodded. "Apparently, he's headed to New York City tonight."

"Are you taking the job?" RJ asked. She finished off her coffee.

"Not sure. I need to talk to Glo. I don't know how soon she wants to go back on the road, or how I feel about protecting another celebrity. But he'd asked me to talk to him after the disaster at the castle, and I agreed."

York took a sip of his coffee. "What if you joined the Caleb group?"

Tate glanced at RJ, then back to York. "Why, are you leaving?"

"No."

"Maybe," RJ said.

York looked at her. Back to Tate. "I don't know what tomorrow will bring. Today, we just need to warn the president."

Tate took a breath. Looked away, nodded. "I hear ya." He met York's gaze. "After Glo's mom was arrested, our world sort of imploded. We weren't implicated, but we needed to be questioned, over and over, about Reba's activities, and Glo really took the whole thing hard, despite the distance between her and her mom. And then, we had to lay low for a long time. But you know, my brother Rueben said something to me that kept coming back to me. And I'm not great at it, but I'm trying."

"What's that?"

"God will keep in perfect peace the man whose mind is committed to Him. Who trusts in Him. And I guess that's just what I'm trying to do."

York nodded. "Me too, I guess."

RJ was looking at him, something in her eyes he couldn't read. Her gaze flickered to the elevator. "Here comes Win." She got up.

Winchester had spiffed up in a pair of black dress pants, a white oxford. He hadn't shaved, but maybe that was on purpose. He wore his sleeves rolled up just past his wrists, showing off a nice Rolex, and a pair of aviator glasses propped backwards on his head.

He came up to them. "Ready?"

Lake stepped up behind him, his usual solemn self.

Ready to tell the president his crazy thesis about Alan Martin, and his possible attempt on his life? Suddenly, the entire thing felt flimsy, half-cocked and like he and RJ had cooked up some Jack Powers plot.

"Yep," RJ said and took his hand.

He managed to nod.

Tate fell in behind them as they walked to a private elevator. A secret service agent stood at the entrance.

York glanced at RJ, gave her a smile. So, their instincts were still firing. Which meant the needle in his gut that Win wasn't out of this game might be accurate.

He blew out a breath as they got in.

RJ took his hand.

He'd met the president just once before, a private meeting after York had helped track down Jackson and her plot. Maybe the man wouldn't even remember him.

The elevator opened to a private lobby, more secret service agents. They were all wanded, then a staffer opened the door.

"Win." President White sat on a red velvet sofa and now

rose to take Winchester's hand. He wore his salt and pepper hair short, and today, a blue suit, the flag pin on his lapel. "Did you get that stain out?"

"I blame you. This is what happens when POTUS shows up to an event unexpectedly. Waiters start dropping cake on me."

"Good thing it was after the awards ceremony. Boris was certainly excited to meet you." He laughed. "I'm glad Grey invited me—I nearly missed the fun. Never a dull moment around you, Win."

He turned to York then. "York. It's been a whole minute." He wore real warmth in his blue eyes. "How are you?"

York stepped forward, nonplussed, and took his hand. "Good, sir."

"And RJ. How are you?" He met her hand.

Then he got to Tate. Poor man stood at attention, probably his military history kicking in. "Sir," Tate said.

"How are you, Tate? And Glo?" He shook Tate's hand, too.

For his part, Tate appeared a little undone. "Good, Sir. And...I'm just glad to see that you're well and—"

"Calm down, Tate. I know you and Glo had nothing to do with Reba's treason. But, if it helps, I forgive you."

And just like that, Tate seemed to breathe again. Except, he closed his mouth and swallowed, as if unable to talk. Instead, he nodded.

President White put a hand on his shoulder, squeezed. "Give my best to your beautiful wife."

Tate nodded.

President White turned back to York. "So, Win says you need to talk to me."

York took a breath. "This is going to sound crazy. But for the better part of the past month, we've been chasing Alan Martin around Europe, and I think he's putting together something big."

President White raised an eyebrow.

"I think he's trying to kill you."

York took a breath, waited, glancing at RJ, then back to the president.

He considered York for a long moment, then turned to a man near the door. "Clear the room, and ask Van to come in here, please." Then he gestured to the sofas. "Sit down, everyone. I'm listening."

He walked over to a chair, and sat, staring at the group as they all sat. Lake stood away, but Win sat next to RJ, crossed a leg over. Tate sat opposite York.

And then York leaned forward and unwound the story, from seeing Alan outside a coffee shop in Paris, to following him to a city in France—

"And this is when your plane was shot down, Win?" President White asked.

Win gave him a thin-lipped nod.

York continued, with details about the attempt on the plane over Sicily, Italy, skipped ahead to the bomb of the CDC director's hotel room at the conference in Florence, then the assassination attempt on Grey's life in Lauchtenland.

"The contract has been withdrawn, and we caught the man who we think took it out—maybe—but he was murdered by, no surprise, Alan Martin."

"Who is still at large," Van Boseman said. He'd come in at the beginning, standing behind them, but now he stepped forward. "What was in the satchel you took from him?" Big man, with dark skin, dark eyes, Van was definitely a man York would want as his security lead.

"Nothing of merit. Money. A key—they haven't found to what. Meds. A few unsavory magazines."

"Any leads on the key?"

"We have a friend—Ziggy—trying to figure that out, but so far, she hasn't come to any conclusions," RJ said.

"Okay. We'll contact Interpol and put out a BOLO on him."

"And Mads Fischer. If that's even his name. But he's also involved, probably on the Russian side," RJ said. "He hired Ruslan to make the bomb. And, forced money out of a Bratva accountant."

Yes, York had left out that part, not wanting to raise any more questions.

Van just nodded. Finally, "What is the reach of this EMP bomb?"

"I'm not sure," RJ said. "But quite a distance if it could take out a plane. And, the device that Ruslan and Mads built is special—it can be focused like a laser on its target. That's what makes it so unique."

"And the unique part of our Boeing 747-200B. The plane is plated in armor that will withstand a nuclear blast, which includes an EMP blast. But, every precaution will be taken."

Van turned to President White. "We need to move your plane to a more secure location. And, move up the time of departure."

White nodded and turned to Win. "Can you leave earlier?"

"No problem."

His words were a fist, right in York's solar plexus. He looked at Win, back to the president. "Win is going with you?"

They had all risen. "Yes. I heard about his personal tragedy last night at the dinner. I offered him a ride home."

York blinked at him, but Tate voiced it. "On Air Force One."

"There's room for you, too, if you'd like."

York looked at RJ, back to President White. Maybe he shouldn't have left out the fact that, well, Win seemed to show up everywhere.

And now, had a red-carpet ride home with the most important man in America.

So, no, York wasn't turning down that ride. "Sure. Thanks."

"Thank you, York. Still a patriot, even on vacation." He shook his hand. "See you tonight. Van will give you all the details."

Van briefed them on the protocols, then let them to the door.

And just like that, it was over, RJ and York standing in the private lobby, waiting for the elevator with Winchester Marshall and Lake.

York looked at RJ, his words gone.

She took his hand.

They stepped into the elevator, rode it down.

It just couldn't be this easy.

"See you guys in a few hours," Win said. "I've got a meeting." He left with Lake.

York turned to RJ. "You feel okay about all this?"

She shrugged. "I don't know. We alerted the president. Interpol can find Martin. And Ruslan is dead, so the CDC director-and you—are safe. I don't know what else to do."

York looked at Tate.

"I hear ya," Tate said. "This whole thing has my gut in a knot. But I need to call my wife."

"It's three a.m."

Tate raised an eyebrow. "You clearly don't know Glo."

York smiled. "Maybe I'm overreacting. Maybe I should just concentrate on my honeymoon."

"Our honeymoon." RJ took his hands. "No more bad guys. Let's get some strudel."

Fine.

Maybe strudel would solve all his problems. York turned with his wife.

And that's when General Boris Stanislov, from Russia, walked into the hotel.

RJ froze. "York."

"I see him."

And York, knew, just knew, this wasn't over.

"I'm missing something."

RJ sat back in the security control room, the footage of last night's charity event in the national ballroom splashed onto four screens. "Can you roll it again?"

She spoke to the German security manager, a man named Cem who had agreed to pull out the tapes after a call to Van netted the okay from the hotel manager.

They'd tried Logan, but for some reason, he wasn't answering his phone. Then again, it was very early morning in D.C. Or wherever Logan was.

Still, with Cem's help, she had started seeing connecting pieces.

"There's Boris, getting his award." She pointed to the screen where General Boris Stanislov, in all his portly glory, received an appreciation award for his efforts to stop global hunger.

Clearly honorary, although President White had received the same award, the same small statue of a woman carrying a basket on her head.

Win had taken a picture with Boris offstage, talked with the man through a translator. She very much wished the footage had picked up their conversation.

Then, Win had sat back down at a table next to President White. Shared a laugh with POTUS.

Meanwhile, a waiter served dessert to the dignitaries' table, which included General Stanislov, President White, and CDC director, Landon Grey.

It was then that the waiter turned, and ran into Win, and spilled the tray onto his lap.

Win jumped up, the cake smearing his shirt, his pants, and while the waiter fussed over Win, she thought she saw—

"Freeze right there."

Yes. She pointed to the screen. "He's putting something in Win's jacket pocket."

York and Tate stood behind her, Cem beside her in the small, dark room, and now York's hand settled on her shoulder. "Well done, babe."

He seemed less rattled than he'd been in the lobby, after their meeting with President White. Helpless. At loose ends.

And if she didn't know it before, she knew it now.

They might, someday, end up in Shelly, Washington, but maybe not.

But the decision didn't have to be up to her. Or to either of them.

I just have to live today, trusting. Being. Saying yes...to the life God wants to give us.

Yes.

"Can you get another angle on that waiter's face?" Tate said.

Cem advanced the footage on the other cameras to match the time stamp. A shot of the stage. A shot from across the room. More cameras in the back of the room. "No."

"Advance them more. I'll bet he turns around," York said.

She slid her hand onto York's and squeezed.

Ten seconds, twenty, the man now bent and picked up plates off the floor. Thirty seconds, forty. Security and other waiters clogged in.

"Nothing," Cem said.

"Keep going," York said.

A minute, too, and it seemed like a rugby scrum, with the staff trying to clean up the mess. President White's security had stood him up, made him and Grey clear away, as did Stanislov's.

Only Win remained, somewhere under that chaos.

And then— "Wait. Look." Tate pointed to the far doors. "That's him."

Cem stopped the tape. Somehow the man had untangled himself from the mess. He had set his tray on a stand near the door, one hand out to push it open.

"Still no clear shot," York said.

"Wait." Cem turned to his computer, chose a setting, then pulled up the picture.

The hallway outside the room. Well lit, with little traffic, a door at the far end.

Cem forwarded the capture to the time stamp on the ballroom still.

Pushed play.

The door opened, and a man stepped out. Turned, fast, toward the door.

Cem stopped it. Backed it up to the moment his face appeared. Maybe he didn't know he was being taped. Or maybe he didn't care.

RJ stilled. "What?"

"You've got to be kidding me." York turned away and blew out a breath.

"What? Who is that?" Tate leaned into the screen.

RJ could describe him with her eyes closed, even without his glasses. Tall, dark-blond hair. "Looks like a viking?"

Tate looked at her, nodded.

"His name is Mads," York said.

"Mads Fischer."

"The guy you mentioned in President White's suite." Tate drew in a breath. "And he's connected how?"

"He's the one who originally led us to the device," RJ said. "I followed him because I thought he was a victim."

"Turns out he was one of the scientists on the project, the one who recruited Ruslan."

"Who built the bomb," Tate said.

"Bomb?" This from Cem.

RJ looked at York. "We need to find out what's in that suit pocket."

York nodded. Turned to Cem. "Where is your dry-cleaning department?"

Ten minutes later, they were sorting through York's suit, freshly cleaned and drying from the cleaning solvent they'd used.

"It's not here," RJ said, after searching through the pockets.

"Maybe he took it out," York said.

"I doubt he knew it was there," Tate said. "If it was planted on him."

"Or, it was supposed to happen that way," York said. "He was right in the way of that waiter."

RJ sighed and handed the suit back to the attendant. She walked out into the hall. "Do we search his room?"

York nodded. "But how?"

Tate smiled. "How about I handle that?" And he headed down to the kitchen.

RJ didn't know how, but he emerged with a universal key card.

"Let's go."

"How—?" RJ quick walked after him.

"I made friends with the busboy who brought up the food for Win. He recognized me. Told him that I forgot my key." He tapped it on the keypad in the elevator and it unlocked Win's floor.

They knocked first, just in case, but Win and Lake were still out.

Even thirty minutes later after they'd gone through Win's clothing, his bedside stand, his toiletries and even Lake's personal belongings.

Nothing that looked like the tiny device slipped into Win's pocket.

"He could have it on him," York said as they left. "And, without knowing what it is, it's hard to pin something on Win."

"I still think Win is innocent here. Someone is using him," RJ said.

Silence between the men. "What?"

"You're just smitten," York said.

"With my cousin?"

"Fan-smitten," Tate said.

Oh brother.

They returned to the lobby, and Tate returned the universal key card.

York got more coffee.

But RJ couldn't stop circling around the puzzle. "Remember when we found Stanislov's itinerary on Ruslan's computer? And Landon Grey's? Clearly, they are here together, and that was important to Ruslan."

"Or Alan Martin," York said. "Ruslan wasn't making much sense when I talked to him."

"But he was coherent before, when he tried to kill me on the boat."

Tate looked at her, his eyes wide. She held up her hand. "Not now.

His jaw tightened.

"What if he was manic-depressive? That can cause an unusual fixation on something right?" York said.

"Maybe." RJ reached out for his coffee.

"And someone who is manic would be pretty focused on getting the job done. He seemed wired when I saw him." He handed it to her.

"You said he was on medication. What if he wasn't?" She took a sip. It seemed to fire her brain.

"They gave him sugar pills?" York took the coffee back.

"Or something like it. What if they just needed him to finish the Marx device, at whatever cost."

"By the time Stanislov saw Grey—"

"Or President White?" Tate said.

RJ looked at him and nodded. "What if that piece was part of the EMP bomb." She stood up. "Like the control board."

"It was small," York said.

"Could be as small as a micro-SD card."

"Easy to hide." Tate had glanced up. "Here comes Winchester."

The man came into the lobby, Lake his shadow. Win carried a gift bag and glanced over at them, frowned. "You guys still sitting here?" He checked his watch. "We leave in an hour."

"What did you buy?" York asked.

A beat, then Win reached in an pulled out an oversized book. "It's a children's book about Neuschwanstein Castle. For my niece."

Yeah, the man just didn't have a bad bone in him.

"Lake ordered us a limo. I'll see you guys down here then."

They offered him quiet goodbyes. Lake glanced at them, then followed Win into the elevator.

An hour later, the fist in her gut hadn't loosened, but clearly, she needed a different perspective. A higher tower.

Which apparently meant Air Force One.

Now this was how to travel home in style. "There's a guest area in the back," said Winchester as they climbed the stairs. They'd already gone through a thorough wand search in the hangar area, in an airport outside the city.

"Where are we going?" RJ asked as the driver headed north out of the city, instead of south, toward Brandenburg International.

"The Air Force always sends two planes, identical, with the president. The second plane is in case of situations like this," Tate said. Something had changed in him after the president's words. A confidence, that she hadn't noticed was missing before. "They probably switched to this plane after our conversation this morning."

"I'll bet that had them scrambling. Transferring all those meals, updating the crew," said Win.

"No. They're always prepared. Maybe not with the meals, but I guarantee that that crew was ready. The only difference is that they are upgrading their passengers," said York. He glanced at Win. "I was security for the American Ambassador to Russia, once upon a long time ago. We rode on Air Force One once, to a conference in Brussels."

RJ had sort of forgotten that he'd been one of the elite secret service people who would give their lives for people like his ambassador, or his president.

No wonder he had a hard time walking away from a plot to assassinate, then, and now.

They'd turned into the airfield, clearly transformed into some place clandestine despite its non-operational status. And there, sitting on the tarmac, the beautiful blue and white bird of the office of the president.

She didn't mind the wanding, the pat down, the examination of her bag. And, when they climbed up the back stairs, she simply ran her hand along the leather seats, speechless.

Tate grinned at her. "Cool, huh? Reba Jackson had her own plane, but nothing like this."

First time he'd talked about her without rancor.

"This is the press area," said a woman dressed in the uniform of the US Air Force. "You're forward of the security area." She led them toward a smaller section with eight large seats and a massive television screen. She indicated the seats. "If you like, I can stow your bag downstairs, in the cargo area."

"No, that's okay," RJ said and tucked it in an area on the sides of the compartment.

"Would you like a quick tour?"

"Really?"

"In the approved areas, but yes. My name is Veronica. Call me Ronie."

"I'll stay here," York said, and Win buckled into a seat at the end, with plenty of leg room. Lake looked like he was staying too, so only Tate and RJ followed Ronie into an area with seats shoved up to small tables. "This is the secretarial, or general staff area." Already a couple people, maybe even interns, sat with their computers open.

Ronie led them down the corridor and stopped. "This is our conference room. The president also uses it for dining." She stepped inside but blocked them from entering. Still, RJ leaned into the room. Armed leather chairs surrounded a massive oval table.

"And next to the conference room is the galley." Ronie let them peek inside where three chefs were packing up food-stuffs. Another chef, also in an Air Force uniform, came up a nearby stairs. "Our food storage, as well as cargo and mechanicals are on the lower floor," Ronie said. "I'm afraid that's as far as I can show you. The rest houses our senior staff as well as the president's office and private quarters. As well as a sitting room and quarters for the secret service personnel.

She ushered them back to the guest area. "President White said he'll invite you back when we're in the air.

RJ sat down next to York and buckled. "Okay. I'm going to stop freaking out now. What's going to happen? The entire plane is highly defended."

York slipped his hand over hers. "RJ. There will always be evil. As Roy said to me a couple weeks ago, our job is to fight the good fight and let God take care of the big picture."

She sighed. "You're right. We've done all we can. Now, we're going to stop overreacting and enjoy the ride."

She leaned her head back and closed her eyes.

And tried to believe her own words.

CHAPTER
TEN

B erlin, Germany

All this sitting around the house this past year had turned Tate into a pansy.

He'd practically broken down and wept when President White forgave him for, well, being so blind he'd nearly let his mother-in-law kill the man.

Yeah, if he were honest, he was a long way from forgiving himself. But White's words helped. And clearly, he meant them because after they'd taken off and leveled off at forty-five thousand feet, Ronie came back and invited them up to the conference room.

White stood with his arms folded, watching a flat screen television, a reporter from Florida, talking about some near tragedy at an air show.

He picked up the remote and turned it off, then turned to

the group. Even Win had decided to join them, although probably, he'd seen it before.

Tate liked Win. He did. But he also couldn't get past the
many, many, many coincidences surrounding Win's appear-
ances in their lives.

But, like RJ and York, he simply liked the guy. So, he didn't
know what to do with his gut instinct that Win was clean.

"Welcome," President White said. "I thought I'd bring you
back now—the pilot tells me we're going to run into some
turbulence once we get over France. I'm not sure how credible
the threat was, but I thank you for all you did to keep me, and
my staff safe."

RJ looked at York, and Tate knew his sister's brain still
replayed the dead-end goose-chase they'd conducted at the
hotel, as well as all the other pieces that didn't make sense.
Frankly, he had a hard time keeping it all straight, but she was
the former CIA analyst in the family. She'd figure it out.

"You kept this silly statue," Win said and walked over to
the statue Tate had seen on the CCTV monitor, the same one
given to Boris Stanislav.

"It's not mine. It's Grey's. Or, rather, it was Grey's. He gave
it to me last night because he said it was my policies that
brought the changes he was awarded for. I turned him down,
but he left it on the table, so I brought it with me in my satchel.
Apparently, he stayed behind for a tour of preparedness facili-
ties at Landstuhl Medical Center Army. I'll have to have my
staff send it to him—"

"You'll have to send it to Russia," Win said. "This one is
inscribed to the general."

White raised an eyebrow, walked over to the statue. Win
handed it to him, and White read the inscription. "Oh, for
pete's sake. I must have picked up the wrong statue." He set it
back on the counter. "Great. Now I've stolen Russian property."

Everyone laughed.

"We'll be home in about seven hours, which is about six a.m. local time. So, try and get some shut eye."

He held out his hand, and York shook it, along with RJ and Win. They followed Lake out of the room. Tate moved to follow.

"Tate. Stay back. I'd like a word with you."

Tate stilled.

Perfect. This was the moment when President White, outside the view of everyone else, turned and accused him of his stupidity for not seeing the obvious. For his blind dedication to a woman who only used him, over and over.

This is where he told him that he was stripping him of any military accolades, and maybe even putting him under investigation—

"Tate, I'd like you to come and work for me."

Tate blinked at him. White had walked up to him, folded his arms, and now leaned against the table. "What?"

"I know you might not like me after everything that's gone down—"

"I like you, Sir."

White smiled. "Okay, I get that you're in my plane, as my guest—"

"No, really, Sir. I voted for you. I believe in you. You're my president."

Aw, see—sappy! He could even feel his face turning read.

White smiled.

Tate just wanted to take a dive under the table.

"Okay, sit down, Tate and hear me out."

"Yes Sir."

"You can call me Isaac."

"I don't think I can Mr. President." Tate sat in one of the wide, luxurious padded chairs.

White sat down opposite him. "I have put together a small, private, powerful, but off the books security team that looks into particular threats around the globe."

Tate's eyes widened, but he shut his mouth. No need to give away York's confidence.

"It's run by a former SEAL, a man named Logan Thorne. You might have met him back when...well, when everything went down with Reba."

He nodded, the name familiar.

"Also on the team is a man named Roy Benjamin, also a former SEAL, and a couple others whose names I can't disclose, given their undercover status."

He nodded.

"My team could use someone who knows close protection like you do. I know Winchester interviewed you for a position on his team, and I don't like to poach a man, but...if I could entice you to join our team, we're small, but we do mighty things." He leaned forward. "Things the world will never know, and probably shouldn't, if they want to sleep soundly in their beds at night."

Tate swallowed, nodded.

"I know you were a Ranger, Tate. I read your jacket. I know about Afghanistan. About the personal trauma, the losses, and your own run in with the Petrov Bratva."

Oh. He nodded.

"If you feel any hesitation about going against these guys again—you know how ruthless they can be, and in full disclosure, they're the current number one enemy of our country. Yes, we have terrorists, and threats to our economy, and possible biological terrorism, but at the heart of it seems to be this group who feels like the world would be a better place if they were in charge." He leaned back. "I disagree. But I can't disagree alone. Which is why I formed this group." He took a breath. "We're more clandestine than we are spec ops, but we could use a man with your spec op skills, and your close protection history. But if you have any hesitation, then I totally understand. That wife of yours took a blow, and if you want to say, Isaac I've done enough for my country, thank you so much, but I pass, I'll understand."

Tate nodded. "Thank you, Sir."

"You'll want to talk to your wife about it."

"Can I, Sir?"

"Yes. But we would like her to keep it to herself."

"Yes, Sir."

"No hope of Isaac?"

"No, Mr. President."

White laughed as the plane shimmied, jerked. "Turbulence. Maybe it's time to buckle in."

Tate got up. "Thank you again. I will talk to Glo and get back to you as soon as I can. I...don't know what to say, really. I never thought—"

"Keep your eyes forward, Tate. Not on the past. You'll never get anywhere looking behind you."

The plane jerked again on his way back to the guest area, and weirdly, Glo's song entered his head. *Brand new day, brand new life...*

He got to the guest area and noticed York sat alone.

"Hey," he said, sliding into the seat across the aisle. "Where's RJ?"

"She went to the bathroom."

"White says we need to buckle."

York looked at him. "Is that all he said?"

Tate frowned, then, "Wait—do you know something?"

"I know that I gave my brother-in-law a pretty good endorsement to my boss."

"Logan Thorne?"

"President White."

Tate smiled. "Thanks, bro."

York grinned, leaned his head back and closed his eyes.

And Tate sat there and tried to figure out how to tell his wife that he wanted to be a spy.

Probably she shouldn't have eaten that delicious but deadly Caesar wrap from the deli as they'd left the hotel because it sat in her stomach and festered.

And an hour into the flight, it wanted to come back up.

She pressed her hand against her stomach as she exited the bathroom. The plane lurched, and she grabbed an empty seat nearby.

So, perhaps she'd just sit a moment, in case she had another scare.

The plane back here was empty of press, so maybe people didn't care about an international symposium on world pandemics. Security sat further up. No one would see her turn green if things went south.

She dug out her phone, and saw that she'd received a message from Coco. Probably before they'd taken off, and she hadn't noticed it.

Coco>>Good morning. Sorry I missed your text. Yes, I believe Lake has been at that hotel before. Maybe with Winchester. I'm sending you a picture from last year.

The text picture hadn't loaded.

RJ turned on her Wi-Fi and logged into the guest option on the Air Force One internet.

Then she pulled up her text.

The picture was still loading, but she texted Coco back.

RJ>>You're never going to believe this. I'm on Air Force One.

She sent the text, looked out the window. Night had descended upon the plane, but they were high enough to see stars.

Her phone buzzed. Coco had responded.

Coco>> Seriously? How?

RJ>>Long story. Win knows the president. Hooked us up with a ride home.

Coco>>You live a glamourous life while I sit in my pajamas. Did you get the picture?

RJ>>It's loading. But I'm chasing something I can't figure out. While at a charity event, Mads slipped something into Win's suit pocket. He doesn't seem to have it—and we can't find it. But it looked like a microchip.

Coco>>Could be a circuit board.

RJ>>Why?

Coco>>Mads. EMP Bomb. Not sure why he'd give it to Win, but there are four parts to an EMP bomb, right? The power storage—the Marx device that Mads and Ruslan built. A trigger, like a cell phone. A control board. And an antenna, or diffuser that will output the power. But, why give it to Win? Maybe that's just not enough coffee talking.

The plane rattled again, and RJ grabbed the seat.

RJ stared at her phone. Heard Van's voice. *The plane is plated in armor that will withstand a nuclear blast, which includes an EMP blast.*

But what if the blast came from inside the plane?

No. They'd all been searched.

Still.

RJ>>Is it possible to assemble the device if all the parts were smuggled onto a plane?

Coco>>Maybe. If you had all the pieces. But you'd have to be clever about how you'd smuggle them onto *Air Force One*.

Her stomach gurgled again. She was about to get up, to head again to the bathroom when she spotted a man moving toward the stairs down to the cargo area.

Lake. And he carried a bag. She spotted Win's oversized castle book in it.

It was a big book. Maybe it didn't fit under Win's seat. Lake was probably storing it downstairs in the cargo area.

She returned her gaze to the picture on the text. It was still loading. Probably, they throttled the guest logins to preserve bandwidth for the security communications upstairs.

Four parts to an EMP bomb. The power storage. Well, that was the purpose of the Marx device—which, to her recollection, was a cylindrical tube of coils.

She closed her eyes, pressing on her stomach, sorting through the pieces.

What if the overlapping itineraries weren't about the symposium, but the charity event? Putting General Stanislov and the CDC director in the same place?

Then why try and kill the CDC director?

Words from their meeting with White shifted through her head. *This is what happens when POTUS shows up to an event unexpectedly.*

So, he wasn't supposed to be at the Charity event. But Grey was.

But if Grey hadn't been there, then White would have definitely gone to accept his award. Sat at the table with General Stanislov.

Oh, for pete's sake. I must have picked up the wrong statue.

Win, picking up the award sat now in her head.

A statue that Grey had tried to give him. One that the president had simply dropped into his briefcase. Maybe hadn't even been scanned.

A cylindrical statue of a woman with a basket on her head.

Wait—

The plane jerked again, shimmied, but she grabbed the seat and found her feet.

Maybe Grey intentionally left his statue on the table. Or, it was taken during the scuffle, the other left at White's plate.

Whatever the plan, it was now aboard Air Force One.

Inside the faraday armor that would protect the electronics.

But they still needed a trigger. And a fairly large antenna.

She headed toward the stairs.

The trigger was easy—a cell phone. But the antenna—

She stopped at the top of the stairs.

Win's book. It was large enough to hide a flat array antenna, a multiple diode antenna used to point in a wide angle.

Her stomach gurgled again. The wrap or the truth, she didn't know, but she might be ill at the terrible picture she'd put together.

Win, at the center of a plot to take down Air Force One?

She glanced ahead, and could clearly see his head over the seats, a pair of Bose headphones connecting him to the movie on the flat screen.

For a moment, she saw herself yanking the headphones off his head, and demanding the truth.

And then it clicked.

Lake.

Her knees nearly buckled.

Lake had been at the coffee shop. In Tuscany, as they'd discussed plans to get Grey. In Lauchtenland at the event where—

Where York was nearly killed.

Lake was at the club in Prague, had jumped out of a plane with them in Munich, and been the one to alert Declan to her presence at the castle.

Lake might have even pointed Win toward the hotel in Berlin, where the president happened to be staying.

Which meant, what—that he was privy to the president's schedule?

Or maybe...Landon Grey's schedule?

Was he in league with Ruslan? Or—and the plane jerked again, and she grabbed the railing—*Alan Martin*?

And now she was going to be sick. What if he knew about the hit on Grey?

Or...

Her feet hit the landing. Was he the one who put the hit out on York?

But how did he get money from Win's private account?

She glanced down at her phone—

The hand grabbed her, jerked her out into the cargo area.

She dropped her phone, grabbed his wrist, trying to pry his grip off her arm.

Lake. She'd never really taken a good look at him before—he was always just in the background. Although, she did remember seeing him in Paris. Dark hair, glasses. A nondescript, albeit good-looking American in line at the coffee shop.

Right before Win bumped into her and set everything into motion.

"You're hurting me."

"Sorry. Turbulence. It looked like you were going to fall." He let go. "What are you doing down here?"

And right then, her puzzle shattered. What was she thinking? Lake was Win's closest, most loyal bodyguard. He wouldn't try to kill him. Besides, Lake had been a marine. He'd served with the secret service...

She stared at him. "Lake. Who did you protect before you started protecting Win?"

He blinked at her.

A beat passed. Another.

Her gaze went to a backpack against the wall, on the floor. No, not a backpack.

A parachute.

She looked up at Lake. His mouth had turned to a grim line. "Aw, I knew we'd eventually come to this moment."

What—? "You served with Jackson!"

He reached out to grab her, and his fingers connected with her throat. "I'm sorry, RJ. I really liked you. And if you'd left everything alone, it wouldn't have to be like this."

No. It *wouldn't* be like this.

She brought her arm up, then hit him, right in the well of his neck.

He jerked back, and she followed by turning, hard, and slamming her hand down on his arm.

His grip ripped off her.

She bolted for the stairs, but he grabbed her arm.

She turned, braced her other hand on the stairwell, and kicked.

Bam! Her foot slammed his jaw. He let her go, falling back, but the force of it landed her on the cargo deck.

He blocked the exit with his body.

She scrambled to her feet, launching herself down the alley, along the luggage, toward the galley, the other stairs.

"Oh no you don't!" He took off, just steps behind her.

She grabbed a suitcase, whipped it down behind her. It bounced on the deck and he swore, trying to get over it.

Pulling down another, then another, she built a small barricade.

"You won't get away! No one will. The device is already set!" He threw away the bags, fighting through them.

She turned, two hands on the handle of an oversized bag. Too late now to give up. "I'm such an idiot! You took down Win's plane so you could get here, on Air Force One! You knew he was friends with White!"

"Of course I did." He plowed past a bag, just as the oversized one went down. "It was almost too easy." He scrambled over another bag. "But no, I took out the plane for personal reasons. I have Win to thank for getting us here."

"You used him."

"You think I'd actually protect a guy like Winchester Marshall?"

Oh. And she didn't know why she felt a little slapped.

She backed up.

Lake came at her. "For the record, this is all your fault, because if you hadn't ended up at the coffee shop, Martin wouldn't have lost his mind and decided to add some personal vengeance to the master plan."

"You mean York." The plane was still shaking, and she grabbed webbing to stop herself from falling.

Run. Don't talk! But she couldn't stop herself. "He took out the hit on York—"

"No, I did. I needed Alan to focus on the big picture. Getting Gray to cooperate."

He too had grabbed the side when the plane jerked. Now, he plowed forward.

"He didn't, did he? That's why you were going to kill him."

"He came around."

Yes, after he'd seen an assassin go after her husband.

An assassin Lake had hired. She wanted to ask him how,

but maybe it didn't matter. Not when he bent down, then pushed the bag right at her.

The heavy bag hit her, and she stumbled back. Her hand grabbed another bag, and it tumbled down.

But she fell anyway, hard, on her hip.

And Lake was there.

She slapped at him, then curled herself into a ball, kicking hard. "Stay away!"

But his hands were back on her throat. "Go to sleep, RJ. It'll all be over by the time you wake up."

No, no— her hands wrapped his wrist, fighting to rip it away. But he had iron fingers. *C'mon, RJ, think!*

She brought her knee up, hard, and he grunted, but his grip only tightened. Her air had started to cut out.

Don't. Panic.

But frankly, she had nothing but panic.

She clawed at his grip even as the world turned to shadow.

No. Not like this.

Except, maybe—

She closed her eyes, and went limp.

He held her a little longer, but in a moment, let her go. She slumped, the fight over.

Managed to stay limp as he dragged her across the cargo area, past the luggage and down to the galley supply area.

Tried not to jerk when he opened the cooler.

No. This was not happening.

She came to life and kicked him in the knee, scrambled to her feet and took off for the door, pulling down a rack of dishes. They shattered on the floor.

He tackled her right onto the floor, three steps before the stairs to the kitchen.

She landed with such a thump, the world turned hazy.

It cleared when the door closed with a soul-spearing click.

"No!" She got to her feet, pounding on the door. "Lake! No!"

Down here, the plane roared, so she couldn't know if he walked away, but she kept pounding. "Lake!" Stupidly, she tried the handle.

Of course he'd locked the door from the outside.

She slumped down on the floor, the chill of the refrigerator, weaving through her jeans, raising gooseflesh. Good thing she'd changed out of her dress before the flight—that would slow down the hypothermia. But, now what?

Her breath formed in the chilly air. Around her, shelving held pre-prepared meals.

She put her hands to her face.

What. An. Idiot. She should have seen it sooner.

Her thoughts unraveled all the places Win had been, with Lake, standing unobtrusively in the shadows. All the things Lake overheard. All the secrets he harbored.

If he worked for Jackson, then that's how he met Alan Martin. Maybe Alan roped him into the plot, which was why he was at the coffee shop. Maybe to give Alan the flight information.

So Ruslan and Abu could take the flight down with the EMP device they'd taken from Mads. Only, they hadn't taken it.

So, why had they taken Mads? Unless Mads went rogue.

He *had* tried to stop them from taking down the passenger plane in Italy. Or, had he? In the end, he'd swum back to the boat.

She drew up her knees. It didn't make sense.

Unless...unless Mads didn't want them to take down Win's plane. Or the plane in Italy. Unless Mads wanted to save the device for the big picture—Air Force One.

But Alan had to test it somehow, on a bigger, faster, higher plane.

And when it didn't work, of course they had to get it on Air Force One.

To kill the president.

It wouldn't be hard to figure out where White would be. Or how to get on the plane, or even how to smuggle the pieces aboard.

But why the Russian switch?

She closed her eyes, leaned her head back against the door, shivering. Well, that was easy—after the American president was dead, they could track the plot back to a certain Russian general.

And Jackson's original game would be back on track.

She stared at her whitening hands, her breath in the air and tried not to cry.

This was not how the epic adventure of RJ and York was supposed to end.

Around her, the massive plane rumbled. Still, despite the noise, she weirdly heard her brother's voice. *God will keep in perfect peace the man whose mind is committed to Him. Who trusts in Him.*

Maybe that's what this whole adventure had been about, frankly. Trusting God, not just for the end game, but for every step. When she couldn't see her next step, when it all threatened to wash over her, pull her under.

When all she could see was darkness.

Yeah, well hopefully before she froze to death.

Or, before Lake set off his EMP bomb in the mechanical room, took out the flight controls and plunged them all in the ocean.

The name of the LORD is a fortified tower; the righteous run to it and are safe.

Her eyes lifted to the shelving.

And beyond that, in the roof, she spotted a vent.

Now, that's what she was talking about.

Somewhere over Germany

The problem was, none of this was actually over.

York sat in his seat, staring out the window into the dark night, his gut tight, painfully aware that they'd solved exactly nothing.

Nothing.

They didn't know who tried to kill Grey. Or why someone tried to slip Win some tiny SD card.

They did know the target, but even that had been avoided without a problem.

And most of all, he still didn't know who had taken out a contract on him.

Except, maybe, Winchester, also he agreed with RJ.

The man sat in his seat, watching some thriller with Chris Pine in it.

Tate sat on the other side, next to the window, his seat reclined, his eyes closed.

So apparently York was the only one still wound up about... whatever. Maybe he needed a nap, too.

The turbulence rocked the plane, and he turned to see if RJ might be returning from the bathroom. She hadn't been feeling well as they took off.

Nothing.

He closed his eyes, but Tate's words to him kept returning. *God will keep in perfect peace the man whose mind is committed to Him. Who trusts in Him.*

Okay, right. But not easy for a man who spent his life trusting in himself. But maybe that was the point. Who, willingly, let go of his own way and turned it over to God, unless he was face first with his own helplessness?

Like now.

York ran a thumb and finger through his eyes. *Okay, Lord. I trust you. Please sort this all out.*

"Sir?"

He opened his eyes. Ronie stood at his aisle. "Would you like dinner? It's cordon bleu, a salad, fresh bread and asparagus."

"Please."

"And the lady?" She gestured to York's empty seat.

"I think so, but better wait and ask her."

"Yes, Sir." She turned and tapped Win on the shoulder, probably inquiring about the same thing. York took out his phone and opened his texting app. Sent a text to RJ.

York>> Dinner is on the way. You want something?

He waited for the message to be delivered, but it stayed in the sent status.

But, even as he waited his phone buzzed in his hand. Ziggy. He hadn't realized he could get calls up here. But, of course he could.

"Hey," he said.

"Hey there. I thought I should let you know that we tracked down that key. Where are you—it sounds loud."

"Air Force One."

A beat. "Seriously."

"It's a long, but not exciting story."

"Well, mine is a little more exciting. The key had a 'do not duplicate' on it, with the listing of a locksmith. I looked up the locksmith, and he connected the key to a flat not far from your hotel."

"Was it Ruslan's flat?"

"I don't know. Probably. Because we found some interesting things there."

"Like?"

"A program to the charity event Marshall attended. And in the trash, casting pieces of pottery."

He had nothing.

"But most importantly, we found Mads' body."

He stilled. "What?"

"Yeah. Executed."

"Was it the Orphans?"

"I don't think so. He was shot in the head. No Orphan marking. But, he does have a Bratva star tattooed on either side of his shoulders."

"That's high ranking Bratva," he said.

"Yep," Ziggy said. "There's more, York."

"Please tell me you found Alan Martin."

"Sorry. But a body did wash up in the Spree river this morning."

"Who?"

"CDC Director Landon Grey."

He stilled, hollow. "What?"

"Yes. Also killed, execution style. The coroner here says he'd been dead maybe six hours, max."

"So he was killed right after the charity event."

"Looks like it."

He looked at Win, who had put on his earphones. "Do you think you could get the hotel to look and see when Winchester returned to his room that night, and if he left again?"

"Already done, York. Yes, someone left, but it wasn't Win."

His breath caught. "Lake."

"Yes. He left after Win returned to the room. Came back two hours later, after two a.m."

He glanced over. Lake had left shortly after RJ.

Hadn't yet returned.

"Okay, does the president know about Grey?"

"I called Roy, but he's not picking up. He and Thorne are into something in the US, so neither one is currently answering. So, I called you."

"Right. Good. I'll inform the president. Thank you, Ziggy."

"Glad to help, York. Stay alive for a while, okay?"

He laughed. "You too."

He hung up. Glanced back toward the bathroom. RJ still wasn't out.

Unbuckling, he got up and headed over to Tate. Sat down next to him.

Tate opened one eye. "What?"

"Landon Grey was found dead this morning."

Tate sat up. "What?"

"Washed up in the Spree river. And Ziggy did some sleuthing—Lake left the hotel last night after midnight, after the charity event, and came back a couple hours later."

Leaning past him, he shot a look toward Win, then back to York. "He's gone."

"Yeah."

"Should we tell Win?"

"I think we should tell the president, first."

"But we might need Win to get to him."

York glanced at him. Shoot. "Right. Okay."

He got up and sat down next to Win. The man looked at him, then sighed and stopped his movie. Removed his earphones. "Ten minutes left. You know this is right where they get the bad guy."

"I'm aware. And we need your help."

"Doing what?"

"Talking again to President White." He sighed. "We have reason to believe that Lake is up to something...not good."

Win blinked at him. "What is with you? First me, and now my personal security. Lake has three years in the secret service as a Marine. He is loyal and—"

"He was with the secret service?"

"Yes. Got out last year and came to work for me. Highly recommended."

"By whom?"

Win folded his hands together. "Um. By. Well—oh yes, a man named Tom Crowley. Used to work for the CIA."

York couldn't breathe. "Crowley was the mastermind behind VP Jackson's plot to kill President-elect White."

Win just stared at him.

"Crowley was also my former father-in-law, and tried to kill me, and RJ."

"I don't understand."

"Lake is a part of the rogue CIA group *still* trying to kill the president."

"Oh. I..." He looked around. "Where is he?"

"Very good question. A better one is where was he last night between midnight and two a.m."

"I believe he was in our suite."

"Nope. He was out killing Landon Grey."

Win just blinked at him. Then he took off his headphones and got up. "Okay."

York rose. "Okay?"

"I'm going to see if I can talk to Isaac." He pushed past York. "Stay here."

Not on his life. And Tate must have had the same thought because he got up and followed York following Win.

Who ignored them, and walked up to Ronie, heading their direction with a tray of food. "I need to talk to the president."

She raised her eyebrows. "I don't think that is possible. He's retired for the night."

"Then how about Van, his head of security," York said.

Win glanced at him, then nodded. "That would work."

"I saw him in the galley," she said. "He's picking up the president's tray."

Win headed down the hallway, followed by Tate.

But something stopped York. A feeling, maybe, but a glance down the hallway still didn't reveal RJ and frankly, it bothered him.

Tate could brief Van.

York headed down the hallway to the bathroom. Knocked on the door. "RJ? Are you in there?"

Nothing. "RJ!"

Again, no answer. Maybe he should get Ronie to let him in.

He took a breath and headed back down the aisle.

The plane jerked again, rattling hard, and he grabbed the nearest seat. Righted himself.

And his gaze fell down the nearby stairway, the one that led to the cargo area.

A phone lay on the landing.

He ran down the steps and scooped it up.

A picture filled the screen. One of Lake and...a woman. Pretty, redheaded, she was laughing, her arms around Lake's shoulders. He was kissing her arm.

Yeah, they were intimate.

The picture came from Coco. He scrolled down and read her text.

Coco>> That's Lake and a woman named Brielle. Winchester Marshall's assistant. She died in the crash.

Then, two more texts, minutes apart.

Coco>>You still there?

Coco>>I did some checking. Brielle is ex-CIA.

He should have guessed that. York pocketed the phone. Maybe she'd gotten too close to Lake and his plans.

Or maybe she was in on them.

Regardless, Lake had gotten Win's account information from her, York was sure of it.

Which meant Lake had taken out the contract on him.

He walked into the cargo area. "RJ?"

The engines rumbled the entire plane and drowned his voice.

But—good girl—she'd left a trail of luggage.

He ran down the aisle, toward the other stairs, and nearly ran into Van, Tate and Win, scrambling down the stairs.

"She's in the freezer!" Tate said pushing past Van into the storage area, straight to the freezer, pulled the pin blocking the door and opened it.

RJ ran out, practically into Tate's arms.

He pulled her up, walked her back, out of the freezer. She shivered violently.

Tate put her down and York swept her up into his arms. She put hers around his neck, buried her face in his chest. Her teeth chattered. "It...was...Lake—"

"I know. I know. He killed Landon Grey."

She looked up, her eyes wide.

"Ziggy called. But—how did you know?"

"He...he smuggled an EMP device...onto...the plane."

Her words fell, and for a second the plane simply gobbled them up.

Then she pushed away from him. "Did you hear me?"

"He smuggled what—" Van said.

"An EMP Bomb!"

Van's eyes widened. "Where—How?"

"In pieces—Boris's award statue, Win's book, a tiny circuit board he got from Win's suit, and a cell phone. They all create a small, but effective EMP device and my guess is that he's put it

190

somewhere near the computer that controls the flight control system of this plane.

"No, that can't be right. Our communications center is secure—"

"The flight systems, Van. The systems that control the ailerons, flaps, landing gear and fuel system—everything the pilots need to keep us in the air is controlled by a computer. Which is not located in the cockpit, but in the mechanical room at the back of this plane!"

York looked at her. His wife had recovered quickly. Or maybe it was just her panic heating her core.

His, too. "We need to find Lake."

"No, we need to find that device," Tate said.

Van stilled. "My responsibility is to the president. He needs to be ready to evacuate the plane. I'll get the security team hunting for Lake—"

RJ took off.

Right.

Van turned and ran up the stairs.

Tate ran after RJ.

York followed them, around the galley storage, down the cargo area, all the way to the back of the plane, secured with a thick metal grate.

"This is a faraday cage," she said. "But it won't help if the device is inside there."

"How did he get it in there," Tate said.

Through the grating, the components of the plane glowed red, orange, blue.

"He got in there with him," RJ said, and pointed through the cage to a man in an Air Force uniform slumped on the floor, blood pooled around his body, a shot to the head evidencing the coercion. His key card was still attached to his uniform. "My guess is that he was the security down here."

The plane suddenly started to descend, so quickly that they were practically lifted from the floor. York grabbed her, pulled her against him, one hand on the cage.

"That's not turbulence!" Tate said.

"That's an emergency landing protocol," said York. "They're taking this plane to the ground."

Hopefully before an EMP bomb could take them out.

"They won't get there in time!" a voice shouted. "I just have to press send!"

Lake advanced out of the cargo area and stood five feet away—far enough that launching at him would earn him a bullet to his head. "You get that gun from the security guy you killed?"

Lake wore a parachute pack, still unclipped around his chest. "

The plane shuddered, lurched, and York banged against the cage.

"Lake—stop," York said. "Why would you do this? Join the Russians to kill our president?"

"I'm just the guy who gets the job done. Just like you, Voron."

York let the name bounce off him. Probably Martin had told him. But yes, once upon a time, he did get it done.

Now, he hoped God had taken the wheel. Although York was certainly here to help.

The plane continued to descend, fast, and Lake took a step back, even as York and Tate held onto the cage.

"Step away from the cage." Lake lifted the gun on them.

"Not a chance!" RJ said.

Oh, honey, please stop—

"You just can't quit, can you, York? No wonder you drive Alan crazy. Hands up, behind your head."

York complied. "I'll be happy to haunt you, too."

"Okay, this isn't going to be hard. I don't want you on this plane."

Then Lake pointed the gun at RJ. "Smart. Shouting through the vent."

So that's how they found her.

"York. Tate. There's an exit door by the stairs. I'd like you two to disembark."

York just looked at him. "You've got to be kidding."

"Now!" He advanced, his gun nearly to her head. RJ closed her eyes.

Aw. York turned, fought his way against the weight of gravity and headed toward the door, his brain churning.

He could grab Lake, and if he went over then, fine—

"Open it!"

He glanced back. Lake had pulled her to himself, his arm around her neck. RJ still had her eyes closed.

"We'll lose cabin pressure! We're too high—we'll need oxygen!"

If possible, the pilots pushed the plane into an even steeper descent, and everyone fell back, stumbling—

Tate used the angle, whirled around, and swept out RJ's legs.

She fell away from Lake, and Tate kicked him in the face.

Lake spun and fell.

Around them, suitcases tumbled along the floor, most of them bumping up against the far stairway.

The plane jerked, passing through hard turbulence, and York caught himself before the wind took him.

RJ scrambled away, toward the faraday cage.

Tate had fallen, too, with the angle and force of his kick, and must have injured himself, because he stayed down.

York forced himself off the wall, away from the door, got a running start and leaped on Lake.

They rolled, over and over, and hit the luggage area, York on the bottom.

Lake ripped out of his grip, turned and shouted at York.

The roar of the engines ate it. Whatever he said, he turned and scrambled uphill toward the open door.

York grabbed his legs, worked his way up and gripped the pack.

Tore it off him. He threw it away, across the room.

It spun, hit the far wall, near RJ.

That's when he noticed her reaching inside the cage, her arm just thin enough to reach through the grate. *Keep trying, Syd*—

He put his gaze on Lake just as the man rolled and kicked York in the shoulder.

Heat flashed, but not enough to slow him down.

He scrambled up—

"York, look out!"

Lake had scrambled up, still holding the gun. He raised his weapon at RJ. "Open the door!"

York met Lake's eyes, breathing hard, debating simply rushing the guy. Because all that mattered was that RJ—and yes, the president—lived—

Tate took Lake down just as the shot fired.

For a second, the plane bucked, maybe going through a pocket of turbulence, but in that second, Lake rolled off Tate.

Blood ran from Tate's shoulder.

"Tate!" RJ shouted, but he held up his hand.

Lake was heading toward his chute.

York roared and grabbed him, yanking him down to the deck. Got his hand around the gun.

Another shot pinged off the side of the plane. It shuddered with the force of the wind.

And then the plane banked.

They all rolled across the floor. A few suitcases tumbled across the deck. York planted his feet into the cargo floor, finding the ridges.

It slowed him enough, and suddenly the plane righted.

And continued its descent.

And right then, Lake released the door.

The wind stole it right off the hinges, the air swooshing into the cabin. It roared, and with it, the plane shuddered.

They must have descended twenty thousand feet maybe more, because York spotted mountains in the distance.

Lake leaped for the chute, and York was back in the game, clawing at him as the chute went spinning across the floor.

Lake rolled, and York caught his wrists, fighting for control of the gun. Next to him, Tate got up, and tried to help, but his knees buckled.

Tate hit the deck, one hand out, clearly more hurt than he admitted.

The plane bucked again, and the gun jerked out of Lake's grip and slid across the deck, landing near the open door.

York rolled to his knees, scrabbling after it.

A kick to his jaw, sent him backwards. He landed with a thud, his breath nearly out.

Lake leapt for the gun.

Shouts lifted behind him, and York spotted security coming down the far stairs.

"She got it!" Tate's voice rose over the roar of the wind. He clamored toward her.

RJ swiped the key card into the lock. The cage opened.

Tate pushed inside.

But RJ turned to find York's eyes.

He was fighting to his feet, his gaze not on Lake, but on the woman he loved, the one who knew how to keep up, believe in him. Inspire.

Then, her eyes widened.

He turned, and Lake had finally gotten his grip on the gun. And, was pointing it at RJ.

No.

Absolutely not. *Never.*

It was more instinct than thought however, that launched York at Lake.

His body connected with Lake's as the shot went off, but it didn't slow their momentum. Instead, he peddled hard, fast and—

Just like that, they were out of the open plane door.

CHAPTER
ELEVEN

What. Just. *Happened.*

RJ froze, staring at the space York had just been.

Just. Been.

What—?

And then it clicked in.

York. Falling.

And there was no coming back from the dead this time.

She stopped thinking. Just moved. She was already running when she scooped up Lake's backpack.

Pulled it on, buckled the straps, still moving.

"RJ, stop! *Stop!*"

But just how was she supposed to stop when—well for better or worse.

And she wasn't going to let death part them.

"You can't—"

"I can!" She turned to Tate, her feet not stopping. "Get the bomb!"

Then she flung herself out the door.

The wind burned her eyes. Worse, she couldn't breathe. This high up, she had no oxygen, and shoot she hadn't thought about that. Except maybe they weren't that high up because the ground seemed much, much closer than she'd expected.

Although, still higher than when she'd jumped with Win.

Which, had been tandem. Because she hadn't a clue what she was doing.

But York did.

He'd jumped out of plenty of airplanes in his Marine days.

And there he was, in the position, arms out, legs out, as if trying to slow his fall.

Gotcha.

And maybe it was all those Alias shows, but she clamped down on the scream that wanted to release, clamped down on her arms, and legs, kept her eyes on York and flew.

She was falling faster than him, she could tell that much. But she'd have to slow to catch him or she'd pass right by him.

"York!"

Mountains rose in the distance, and below them, beautiful fields opened up over rising and falling hills. Not Munich, but more of rolling fields and it hit her...

France.

She was like Fred. Parachuting into his line to defend Italy. And then going after the person he loved most, regardless of the cost.

"York!"

She was dropping fast, closer, closer—

She opened her arms, her legs—*Please, God*— "York!"

Her hand grabbed his arm and she held on with everything inside her.

He looked over at her, his eyes wide, then reached for her. Pulled her into him, his hands holding her arms.

She patted her shoulder straps, and he nodded. Put his

arms through the shoulder straps. He wrapped his legs around her.

Except. She had no idea where the chute cord was. "I don't know how to pull it!"

He looked down. It looked farther than she'd been with Win, but who was she to judge. It was all a panicked blur.

But not York. He simply removed his arms, and this time inserted them around her, the chute on his shoulders, too. She wrapped her arms around his neck. His legs, he viced around her.

"Ready?"

"Ready!"

He pulled the chute. She looked up, watching, praying—

The smaller one emerged first and pulled the larger chute out of the pack.

It was like a butterfly, finding its wings, unfurling, catching the wind—

It yanked them so hard, she thought he'd drop out from under her. But he'd secured his arms around her, the chute between them, and clamped onto her with his legs and suddenly—

With a whoosh, everything went quiet. The menace of the wind vanished, just the flapping of the chute, the thundering of her heart and...they were drifting.

Drifting, soaring, flying over a glorious landscape. Rolling hills, glorious, jagged mountains in the distance, quaint farmhouses set in green and gold fields.

Breathtaking and serene.

She leaned back, pressed her forehead to his. "Don't let go."

"Never." Then he kissed her. He tasted of the wind, and danger and heat and relief and she just kept kissing him, crying now.

"Hey, hey, we're okay," he said, leaning back. "Look."

She looked down to see houses and fields and cars, all getting larger. "Where are we going to land?"

"I can't let go of you to control it, so I guess wherever the wind takes us."

Which felt exactly right.

They drifted over a barn, toward a grassy field, the world coming faster and closer. "I'm going to put my legs down. So you wrap yours around me, okay?"

He released his legs, and she lifted herself to clamp onto him. And then, just like that, they landed, him holding onto her bottom as he ran to keep them upright, then slowed them and finally, he stopped, breathing hard.

She put her legs down, but they wouldn't hold her.

He caught her before she landed. "You okay?"

"I just need to feel the earth here."

He laughed and lowered her down. She lay in the field, the silk around her, staring at the sky.

In the distance, a trail of white evidenced the planes trek across the sky.

York sat next to her. Then, lay down and stared at the sky with her.

She slipped her hand into his.

"You're a crazy woman, you know that? What if you hadn't caught me?"

"I had to. I didn't know how to open the chute."

He rolled up to one elbow. Just looked at her.

And she looked at him. Those blue eyes, that dark-blonde hair, the way he seemed to drink her in.

"Please never do that again."

"No promises."

He leaned down then and kissed her. Something sweet, soft. But in it, he still trembled. She curled her hand behind his neck, playing with his hair at the nape.

Oh, York.

He finally leaned away. Moisture rimmed his eyes, and he blew out a breath, looked away. Ran his thumb across his cheek.

"You were really scared," she said softly.

His mouth made a grim line. But he nodded. "But not until you showed up."

"You were ready to die? Again?"

"If it meant keeping you safe, Syd."

Now she might cry.

He ran his thumb across her cheek. "How'd you know the EMP device was sneaked onto the plane."

"Oh, I saw all the puzzle pieces in my head, all at once and I knew what Lake was planning."

"He put the contract out on me."

"Yeah. But I still can't figure out how he got the money."

"Brielle. They were lovers. Or maybe partners. But you know what that means?"

"That...a gal has to watch the man she falls for? Or he'll get her in trouble?" She pressed her hand to York's handsome face. He'd taken a couple hits from Lake that left bruises, but then again, when didn't York have a bruise or two?

"No. That I'm free. We're free. No contracts on my life. No ghosts to haunt me." He blew out a breath. "It's over, RJ. It's all over."

Oh. She hadn't realized, really, how much his past haunted him until this moment, when his blue eyes shone clearly, the sun in them, so much light.

"No, York. It's just begun."

His cell phone rang in his pocket.

"I can't believe you have that." She sat up as he pulled it out. Put it on speaker.

"York? Oh geez—" The line turned muffled, but through

the speaker— "He's alive!" He came back on. "RJ? What about—"

"I'm fine, Tater. Breathe."

It sounded like he did just that.

She leaned into the phone. "Are *you* okay? You were shot."

"Yeah. It's just a flesh wound."

She laughed at his Black Knight impression. "Glo is going to kill you."

"Probably. She'll just have to get used to it. Hazard of the job."

Job? "Did you get the device?"

"Yes. And disabled it before it could damage the plane. Good job, sis."

York grinned at her.

Aw shoot, she could admit, saving the world in front of her big brother felt a little good. "Where are you?"

"We just landed at Charles De Gaulle. Where are you?"

"I dunno. Somewhere east of Paris, for sure. In a field."

"We'll come and get you—"

"Nope." York had leaned into the phone. "We've already seen Paris."

RJ looked at him. He grinned at her. "Actually, Tate, we're going off the grid. See, we're on our honeymoon. We'll call you when we get back."

He hung up.

Tossed the phone behind him, onto the silk of the chute.

Then he leaned over her, his arm under her neck, his hand on her face. "Now, where were we before we were so terribly interrupted?"

And when he kissed her, the sky arching blue overhead, the fields around them green, the summer wind caressing them, she knew their adventures were only beginning.

EPILOGUE

How York loved this pristine, autumn day in Shelly. With the perfectly baby blue sky, a few high wispy clouds lazy over the lake, the leaves turning to jewels, and the smell of hickory drifting from his grill on the porch of his forever home, no, nothing could wreck this day.

This life.

He didn't even mind the fact that Roy had tracked him down to his small town hideout, located on lake Wapato, and now sat in an Adirondack chair, nursing a frothy beer, watching York fry up burgers.

"So, I heard about what went down in Florida. We're clear? No other casualties?"

"Seems like it." Roy said, taking a sip.

"I'm sure that's why the Petrovs wanted the President out of the way for their recent attempt to cripple America and draw us into a war."

"You think they'll keep trying."

"Sure of it." Roy shook his head.

"At least now we know why they wanted to take out the plane of African scientists over Sicily. And why the CDC director was involved."

"Yeah. Traitor. Good thing he went down in Germany, or we'd be hunting him, too, no doubt." He looked at York. "Could have been really bad if the Kingston brothers hadn't jumped in to help."

Roy didn't seem any worse for wear, really. He'd gotten a hair cut, shaved, so maybe something official happened he'd had to clean up for.

Or maybe he had plans after this trip to meet up with someone special...

"Haven't met them."

"Triplets. From Alaska. Their family runs a bush plane service."

"How'd they get wind up in a global Russian plot—"

"A woman who landed on their front door, needing help." He glanced at York. "You know a little about that."

York smiled. Yeah, and years later, he ended up with that amazing woman as his wife.

"She worked for the Caleb group, and went missing. The Russians found her about the same time we did. The Kingston brothers are all ex-military, so they could handle themselves. Turned out to be exactly who we needed. I think President White asked one of them to join the C-Group."

"How is Isaac?"

"Glad to be alive." Roy lifted his glass. "If it weren't for—"

"RJ. She's the one who spotted Martin in Paris." York opened the hood of the grill. Smoke poured out and he flipped the burgers, one at a time.

"Okay. Sure. RJ." Roy smiled. "How is she?"

"Good. Feeling better now that she's in her second trimester."

Roy's mouth opened. "Seriously?"

York grinned. From the lake, a couple geese lifted off, squawking.

"Congratulations, pal. What does Anya think about getting a sibling?"

York cast his gaze out to the yard, where Anya swung on the big rope swing he'd attached to the massive black cottonwood. She had one foot on the ground, spinning herself around and around, her head back, her braids flying.

"I think she's good. She seems to be talking more, and RJ is working with the school counselor to help her adjust. She's a fighter."

"Belongs in the family, then."

Yes, she did. And maybe it was crazy to adopt a Russian gangster's granddaughter, but she needed a real home.

And York was building one. "We make it legal in a few weeks."

"Domestic life looks good on you."

York glanced down at the grilling apron. He wore a pair of jeans, a tee-shirt, but more, something inside him had sort of loosened, the hard fisted breath of dread, maybe.

He glanced back at Roy, however, and the expression on his face had his breath tightening. "Spill it."

"Right." Roy set the glass down on the deck and got up. Joined York at the rail, to stare out at the lake. It lapped against the shoreline, the dock already out for the year.

"Alan Martin has turned up."

York stilled, a knot forming in his chest. "Really."

"Yeah. He just murdered one of our agents in Switzerland—"

"Please tell me it wasn't Ziggy."

"She's okay." Roy's jaw tightened.

"What's that look? I thought you two—"

"We're just friends." Roy looked away.

Sure they were.

"But I am worried about her. She's into something that could get her killed."

"So, doing her job." York opened the grill again and checked the burgers. Perfect. He pulled them off and set them on a plate.

Roy glanced at him, nodded. "That's the problem, isn't it? Don't fall in love with a spy."

York picked up the plate to take over to the picnic table on the other side of the deck.

"I envy you, pal. You actually figured it out. How to live in both worlds."

Had he? York set the plate down, next to a pile of buns, a salad, a pitcher of lemonade.

"So far, so good. We set up an office in the basement, and RJ seems happy to chase down the leads there. But we're just taking it one day at a time. One choice at a time. Right now... this feels like a good choice."

He waved to Anya. "Kooshet!"

She got off and came running. RJ must have heard them because the sliding door opened, and she came out, carrying a plate of freshly baked cookies. He resisted the urge to press his hand on her growing belly—very slight so far, but he saw it in her countenance.

Peace.

"So, I guess that's a no for helping me chase down Martin," Roy said, his voice low.

The name stirred an old urge for justice inside him, but he shook his head.

Anya came up to the deck and greeted Roy, in Russian.

RJ set down the cookies.

Then she looked at Roy. At York. And smiled.

"But keep us posted. We're not out of the game. We're just getting more creative."

She winked at York, then pulled out a chair.

"Oh, and hon, don't forget to turn off the grill. We don't want to run out of gas for the next time Roy shows up needing us to save the world."

He glanced at Roy, who was grinning. "Yep."

York walked back to the grill and turned it off. Let the smoke die down as it dissolved into his perfect, blue skied world.

WHAT HAPPENS NEXT...

Thank you for reading this fun, epic trilogy! I wrote it not only because readers were clamoring for more of RJ and York...but also as a way to see a bigger global picture of the epic plot behind the Sky King Ranch trilogy. If you've been reading that series, this is another view of the plot—something that will expand your view of the intrigue that concludes (or mostly!) in Sundown, book #3 of the Sky King Ranch series.

Not sure what I'm talking about? Start the adventure by meeting the Kingston brothers, from Sky King Ranch!

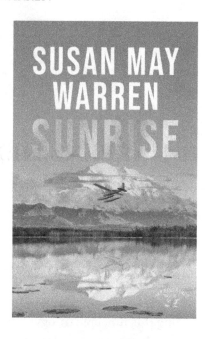

Pilot Dodge Kingston has always been the heir to Sky King Ranch. But after a terrible family fight, he left to become a pararescue jumper. A decade later, he's headed home to the destiny that awaits him.

That's not all that's waiting for Dodge. His childhood best friend and former flame, Echo Yazzie, is a true Alaskan—a homesteader, dogsledder, and research guide for the DNR. Most of all, she's living a life Dodge knows could get her killed. One of these days she's going to get lost in the woods again, and his worst fear is that he won't be there to find her.

When one of Echo's fellow researchers goes missing, Echo sets out to find her, despite a blizzard, a rogue grizzly haunting the woods, and the biting cold. Plus, there's more than just the regular dangers of the Alaskan forests stalking her . . .

Will Dodge be able to find her in time? And if he does, is there still room for him in her heart?

Sunrise is the first explosive volume in a new nail-biting series from *USA Today* bestselling author Susan May Warren
Pick up Sunrise today!

A NOTE FROM SUSIE MAY

Thank you so much for reading *No Matter the Cost!* I hope you enjoyed the story. If you did, would you be willing to do me a favor? Head over to the **product page** and leave a review. It doesn't have to be long—just a few words to help other readers know what they're getting. (But no spoilers! We don't want to wreck the fun!)

I'd love to hear from you—not only about this story, but about any characters or stories you'd like to read in the future. Write to me at: susan@susanmaywarren.com.

I also have a monthly update that contains sneak peeks, reviews, upcoming releases, and free, fun stuff for my reader friends. Sign up at www.susanmaywarren.com

And, if you're interested reading more epic romantic suspense, head over to https://www.susanmaywarren.com/genre/contemporary-romantic-suspense/

Thank you again for reading!

Susie May

ABOUT SUSAN MAY WARREN

With over 1.5 million books sold, critically acclaimed novelist Susan May Warren is the Christy, RITA, and Carol award-winning author of over forty-five novels with Tyndale, Barbour, Steeple Hill, and Summerside Press. Known for her compelling plots and unforgettable characters, Susan has written contemporary and historical romances, romantic-suspense, thrillers, rom-com, and Christmas novellas.

With books translated into eight languages, many of her novels have been ECPA and CBA bestsellers, were chosen as Top Picks by *Romantic Times*, and have won the RWA's Inspirational Reader's Choice contest and the American Christian Fiction Writers Book of the Year award. She's a three-time RITA finalist and an eight-time Christy finalist.

Publishers Weekly has written of her books, "Warren lays bare her characters' human frailties, including fear, grief, and resentment, as openly as she details their virtues of love, devotion, and resiliency. She has crafted an engaging tale of romance, rivalry, and the power of forgiveness."

Library Journal adds, "Warren's characters are well-developed and she knows how to create a first rate contemporary romance..."

Susan is also a nationally acclaimed writing coach, teaching at conferences around the nation, and winner of the 2009 American Christian Fiction Writers Mentor of the Year award. She loves to help people launch their writing careers. She is the founder of www.MyBookTherapy.com and www.LearnHowtoWriteaNovel.com, a writing website that helps authors get published and stay published. She is also the author of the popular writing method *The Story Equation*.

Find excerpts and reviews of her novels at www.susanmaywarren.com and connect with her on social media.

facebook.com/susanmaywarrenfiction

instagram.com/susanmaywarren

twitter.com/susanmaywarren

bookbub.com/authors/susan-may-warren

goodreads.com/susanmaywarren

amazon.com/Susan-May-Warren

CONTINUE THE ADVENTURE

THE EPIC STORY OF RJ AND YORK

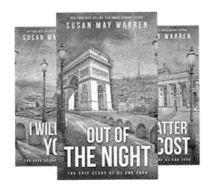

Book 1: Out of the Night

Book 2: I Will Find You

Book 3: No Matter the Cost

ALSO BY SUSAN MAY WARREN

FIND OTHER EPIC ROMANTIC ADVENTURES BY SMW!

Sky King Ranch

Global Search and Rescue

The Montana Marshalls

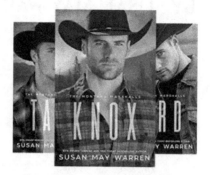

Montana Rescue

Montana Fire

Global Guardians

CPSIA information can be obtained
at www.ICGtesting.com
Printed in the USA
LVHW101448070922
727709LV00004B/454